"WITHOUT A LEADER, THE HORSES WILL RACE IN CIRCLES AND BE SLAUGHTERED!"

Prudence was right. The herd would be lost without the wild stallion to lead them. The plan had gone wrong and now there was nothing, except a blood-bath victory for Egan.

"You could find him, ride him past Egan's men," Skye suggested. "Bring him back here."

"There's a full moon," Prudence pointed out. "They'd see me."

"Not if you were naked and black, as black as the Wild Shadow. . . ." Fargo led her to a mountain stream and started making a mud paste while Prudence slowly undressed.

He smeared the black paste over her face and eyelids, down along her neck and shoulders. When his fingers trailed over her full breasts, Prudence gasped and shuddered. When his hands reached the inside of her thigh, her eyes snapped open and she put her hand over his. . . .

Exciting Westerns by Jon Sharpe from SIGNET

(0451)

☐ **THE TRAILSMAN #1: SEVEN WAGONS WEST**

(110528—$2.25)

☐ **THE TRAILSMAN #2: THE HANGING TRAIL** (110536—$2.25)

☐ **THE TRAILSMAN #3: MOUNTAIN MAN KILL** (121007—$2.50)*

☐ **THE TRAILSMAN #4: THE SUNDOWN SEARCHERS**

(122003—$2.50)*

☐ **THE TRAILSMAN #5: THE RIVER RAIDERS** (111990—$2.25)

☐ **THE TRAILSMAN #6: DAKOTA WILD** (119886—$2.50)*

☐ **THE TRAILSMAN #7: WOLF COUNTRY** (099052—$2.25)*

☐ **THE TRAILSMAN #8: SIX-GUN DRIVE** (121724—$2.50)*

☐ **THE TRAILSMAN #9: DEAD MAN'S SADDLE** (112806—$2.25)*

☐ **THE TRAILSMAN #10: SLAVE HUNTER** (114655—$2.25)

☐ **THE TRAILSMAN #11: MONTANA MAIDEN** (116321—$2.25)

☐ **THE TRAILSMAN #12: CONDOR PASS** (118375—$2.50)*

☐ **THE TRAILSMAN #13: BLOOD CHASE** (119274—$2.50)*

☐ **THE TRAILSMAN #14: ARROWHEAD TERRITORY**

(120809—$2.50)*

☐ **THE TRAILSMAN #15: THE STALKING HORSE**

(121430—$2.50)*

☐ **THE TRAILSMAN #16: SAVAGE SHOWDOWN**

(122496—$2.50)*

*Prices slightly higher in Canada

Buy them at your local bookstore or use this convenient coupon for ordering.

THE NEW AMERICAN LIBRARY, INC.,
P.O. Box 999, Bergenfield, New Jersey 07621

Please send me the books I have checked above. I am enclosing $_____
(please add $1.00 to this order to cover postage and handling). Send check
or money order—no cash or C.O.D.'s. Prices and numbers are subject to change
without notice.

Name_____

Address_____

City _____ State _____ Zip Code _____
Allow 4-6 weeks for delivery.
This offer is subject to withdrawal without notice.

THE TRAILSMAN
17

RIDE THE
WILD SHADOW

by
Jon Sharpe

A SIGNET BOOK
NEW AMERICAN LIBRARY
TIMES MIRROR

PUBLISHER'S NOTE

Copyright © 1983 by Jon Sharpe

The first chapter of this book appeared in *Savage Showdown*, the sixteenth volume of this series.

SIGNET TRADEMARK REG. U.S. PAT. OFF. AND FOREIGN COUNTRIES REGISTERED TRADEMARK—MARCA REGISTRADA HECHO EN CHICAGO, U.S.A.

SIGNET, SIGNET CLASSICS, MENTOR, PLUME, MERIDIAN AND NAL BOOKS are published by The New American Library, Inc., 1633 Broadway, New York, New York 10019

First Printing, May, 1983

1 2 3 4 5 6 7 8 9

PRINTED IN THE UNITED STATES OF AMERICA

The Trailsman

Beginnings . . . they bend the tree and they mark the man. Skye Fargo was born when he was eighteen. Terror was his midwife, vengeance his first cry. Killing spawned Skye Fargo, ruthless, cold-blooded murder. Out of the acrid smoke of gunpowder still hanging in the air, he rose, cried out a promise never forgotten.

The Trailsman, they began to call him, all across the West: searcher, scout, hunter, the man who could see where others only looked, his skills for hire but not his soul, the man who lived each day to the fullest, yet trailed each tomorrow. Skye Fargo, the Trailsman, the seeker who could take the wildness of a land and the wanting of a woman and make them his own.

*1861—the wild mountain basins
of the Absoroka Range where it crosses
the borders of the Montana and
Wyoming Territories.*

She was sweet-faced, almost naked, the mayor's daughter, and in bed with him. She was also the damnedest surprise he'd had in years.

Skye Fargo pushed back black, unruly hair that fell over his forehead and knew that amazement still lined his chiseled, intense face as he watched the girl stretch languorously on the bed. Even clad only in panties, as now, she retained that sweetly innocent air, as though she were a little girl playing grown-up. But her body was very grown-up, all beautifully curved, everything rounded, knees, hips, shoulders, graceful legs, modestly full breasts, everything pink-fleshed, nipples very pink, the circles behind each even pinker.

"What are you thinking, Fargo?" she asked, turning on her stomach, her smile mischievous.

"I'm thinking you've been a helluva surprise from the first day we met, Penny Wills," he said. She giggled and stretched again, and he let his mind go back to that first day. Hell, it wasn't even a week back. He'd brought a wagon of silver ore to the town and been paid well for it. The town wasn't much of a place, an overgrown way station named Threadneedle because it sat between two mountains of the Absaroka Range on a narrow passway. He'd gone to the general store to get himself a new pair of boots, and she'd been there, buying a piece of yard goods, all dressed in pink cotton and a small pink parasol, looking like a stick of curvaceous cotton candy.

"I'm Penny Wills," she'd introduced herself with a bright smile. "Just get into town?" she'd asked, and he'd nodded.

"Strangers are easy to spot here," she'd said. "Especially handsome ones." He remembered taking her in, sensing something under that cotton-candy, sweet-faced exterior. Perhaps men, any men, were hard to come by in Threadneedle, he remembered thinking, and wondering, because it was a town that got a lot of men passing through.

"What do you do with handsome strangers?" he'd tossed out.

"That depends," she said with a quick smile. "Sometimes we go riding or picnicking, sometimes to a hoedown if there is one."

"Kind of hot for a hoedown," he'd remarked.

"Yes, it is hot. I could stand a drink," she'd said, and it had been only the first of the surprises to come.

"I only saw one saloon. You wouldn't want to go there, would you?" he'd said.

"Why not? I'm the mayor's daughter. My father's Humphrey Wills. I can go anyplace I like in this town," she'd said.

They'd had the drink, then another, and he'd walked her to a modest house at the end of town. The rest had followed not only quickly but with effortlessness on his part. They'd gone riding the next day. She'd said she wanted to show him the beauty of the mountain range. She'd shown him a lot more. Once alone in the hills, she'd unbuttoned her shirt and ridden with her breasts out, bouncing merrily in rhythm. "I like the feeling of freedom," she'd said. When they'd stopped to rest, she'd let him caress the pink-fleshed, lovely mounds, but she'd pulled away at anything more. He'd thought then that perhaps she was just a tease, one of those strange women who got their kicks out of tantalizing a man.

Nothing had changed his mind the next day when they went into the lower hills of the Absaroka Range again, only this time her lips had responded with more fervor and there had been little moans as he pressed his mouth to the pink-fleshed mounds. But she'd pushed away again, sat back, her eyes studying him. "You're too handsome to let go by," she'd said. "But I like comfort, a big bed, a warm room, pillows, and privacy. You don't know who might happen along out here."

"Such as Daddy?" he'd asked.

She'd given her little-girl giggle. "There's a little hotel the other end of town. Get a room tomorrow night," she'd said. "I'll come by."

"I'll be there," he'd said. He'd followed her orders with eagerness pushing away surprise, feeling a little like a man who'd fallen into a gold mine. And now he watched her in the little hotel room as she rolled over to him, still keeping panties on. She let one hand move across the naked beauty of his hard-muscled physique, the powerful shoulders and broad chest, the long, rippling muscles of his thighs, and there was appreciation in her eyes.

"God, you're a piece of man," Penny Wills murmured.

He reached for her. "And you're a delicious little surprise package, Penny Wills," he said. He pulled her to him and his hand caressed her breasts. He let his fingers move down across her curvaceous body, neared the dark triangle visible through the thin panties. His thumb

3

hooked onto the edge of the garment, began to push it down, and her hand came at once to stop him.

"Not yet," she breathed. "I have to work up to it. I have to look, touch, feel, first."

He drew his hand away, brought it up to cup her breast, and with unexpected suddenness she threw her arms around him, lifted herself half over him, and he felt his swollenness hard against her belly. She rolled on her back, pulled him with her. "Ah . . ." she breathed. His hand went down to push away the thin panties. Then he heard the door burst open.

"Shit!" he swore, rolled from her, tried to reach the holster beside the bed with the big Colt .45 in it, but the voice froze him halfway across the bed.

"Don't try it, mister," the voice said. Slowly, Fargo turned to see the three figures that had burst into the room, each holding a rifle. He saw Penny pull her dress on with one quick motion as a fourth man strode into the room, pulling the door shut behind him. He fastened Fargo with an icy stare out of a hawklike face.

"You're in trouble," the man said. "You've taken my little girl."

"I didn't take anything, yet," Fargo said.

"In bed naked, laying on top of her, you were. How much more proof do I need?" the man said sternly. "An innocent young girl. You'll have to do right by her, now."

Fargo sat up, frowned at the man. "What the hell does that mean?" he shot back, eyed the rifles again, decided there was no chance to make a move.

"It means you'll marry her, right here and now," the man said. "You violated her and you're going to make it right by her."

"What?" Fargo shouted. "You out of your damn mind?" He stood up, and one of the other men slammed the stock of his rifle into his stomach. He doubled over

4

in pain, fell back onto the edge of the bed, hands to his midsection.

"Call Preacher Tooms," he heard the mayor say. One of the other men opened the door and shouted into the hallway. The preacher appeared at once, dressed in his black frock coat, Bible under one arm, a tall, dried-up looking man. Fargo straightened up, fought down the pain in his stomach.

"Put your pants on," one of the men ordered and watched with the rifle on him as Fargo pulled into his trousers.

"Wed this man to little Penny," the mayor said, and Fargo stood up, backed away from the man who'd slugged him. He saw Penny move to stand a little closer to him, and he stared at her with a frown of incredulity.

"Now just a damn minute," he protested. "You can't do this. She came up here all on her own. Fact is it was her idea."

"A young girl is easily lured into sin by a clever man," Humphrey Wills said. "We're ready, preacher," he said to the minister.

The man opened his Bible. "We are gathered here to join in holy matrimony these two young people," he began, and the mayor broke in brusquely.

"Cut all that and get on with it, Lemuel," he snapped.

The preacher turned a page in the book. "Do you, Penny Wills, take this man to be your lawfully wedded husband?" he read.

"I do," Fargo heard Penny say sweetly.

"Shit you do," he shouted. "You take that back, goddammit." He started toward her, and one of the men with a rifle stepped forward menacingly.

"Do you, Skye Fargo, take this woman to be your lawfully wedded wife?" the preacher went on.

"In a pig's ass," Fargo roared.

"He said 'I do,'" the mayor cut in. "I heard him. You hear him, boys?"

"We heard him," the three riflemen said.

"I pronounce you man and wife," the preacher said, snapping his Bible shut.

"Like hell you do. This is no wedding. This is a fucking farce," Fargo shouted. He watched Penny calmly start toward the door. "Goddamn little bitch," he yelled. "You set me up."

Penny disappeared out the door, and her father's hawk face stepped in front of him. "You are legally married by the powers invested in Preacher Tooms," the man said calmly. "Finish dressing and the boys will bring you to my office." He turned and strode from the room.

Fargo's eyes went to the three men. They held the rifles steady on him, and he watched one pick his gunbelt from the floor, sling it on his shoulder. He gathered up the rest of his clothes and dressed. One of the men gestured with the rifle to the hallway. Fargo walked from the room and felt the one man at his back, the other two falling in on each side.

They walked him from the hotel outside into the night street and a few hundred feet to a small, lighted office. He saw two barred cells behind the front room as he was taken inside. Mayor Humphrey Wills rose from behind a small wooden desk with his name in large letters, the word "Mayor" even larger. "Sit down, Fargo," the mayor said as the three riflemen leaned against the wall. Fargo slid into the chair, glanced at the two cells and saw a man inside one, stretched out on the single cot. Fargo returned his eyes to the hawk-faced man in front of him.

"Now what the hell are you trying to pull off here?" he growled.

"Pull off? You have the wrong idea, Mr. Fargo. You violated my daughter and you had to do the right thing by her. You married her. You've been properly and legally married, by a preacher with witnesses," the man said.

"Proper and legal my ass," Fargo flared.

The man's face didn't change at his angry retort. He continued calmly, and Fargo began to realize it was a speech he had made many times before. "However, because of the powers of my office, and out of the compassion inside me, I can offer you a way out. I can annul this marriage. It will cost you five hundred dollars."

Fargo's lake-blue eyes stayed on the man and he let his lips purse. A small, grim smile slid over his face. "Very nice," he murmured. "Really nice. How long did it take you to dream up this racket?"

Mayor Humphrey Wills stared back calmly. "Five hundred dollars," he said.

"I don't have five hundred dollars with me," Fargo said.

"You came in here leading an ore wagon. You were paid for that job," the man said.

"Three hundred dollars," Fargo said.

"You can give us that. Then you'll only have to spend six months on our work gang," the mayor said.

"Work gang?" Fargo frowned.

"You'll go wherever we send you, into the silver mines if they need extra help, logging camps, wherever," the man said.

"And if I don't pay up anything?" Fargo asked.

The man's hawk face wrinkled in thought for a moment. "I'd say you'd be on the work gang for three years," he replied casually.

"You sonofabitch," Fargo said.

"Five hundred dollars," the man repeated calmly. "Five hundred dollars and you're a free man." He leaned forward in the chair, his face growing harsher. "Let me spell it out more clearly for you. If you try running, every sheriff in every territory will get a notice that you're a runaway husband and wanted here. Every bounty hunter

7

will get a notice of a price to bring you back. And it will be all perfectly legal and within our rights. You'll be a husband who has abandoned his wife, remember." He leaned back in his chair. "By morning, you'll join all the others in my files at home, your marriage legally documented, signed by three witnesses, everything completely in order," he said.

"Bastard," Fargo said.

Mayor Wills leaned forward in the chair, and what passed for a smile crossed his face. "Now isn't it worth five hundred dollars to have all that off your back?" he said. Fargo stared at him in icy silence. "Three years on a work gang is a long time. Even six months," Mayor Wills said. "Most men quickly change their minds and find some way to get the money."

"And the others?" Fargo asked.

The man shrugged. "They're very helpful. Labor is in short supply around here," he said. Fargo felt the fury seething inside himself. "Give us the three hundred," the man said. "Six months isn't so long. Of course, you'll still be married then. You'll still have to come up with the money to have me annul that."

"Go to hell," Fargo said. "And take that pussy-waving little bitch daughter of yours with you."

The caricature of a smile came again. "Put Mr. Fargo in a cell, boys. We'll give him the night to think about his unwise reactions," he said, and Fargo felt the rifle prod him in the back at once. He was pushed into the cell with the man on the cot, the door latched, and he turned to see the mayor drop his Colt and the gunbelt into a drawer in the desk, slam it shut, and lock it. He watched the man turn the desk lamp down low before leaving the little office with the three riflemen. A lock was turned on the door from outside, and the mayor and his helpers disappeared from view.

Fargo turned, saw the man on the cot sitting up, a young face, not more than nineteen, he guessed. "Welcome," the young man said, grim irony in the single word.

2

Fargo leaned against the bars and took in the younger man's boyish face. "What's your name, son?" he asked.

"Chuck Hapgood," the boy said.

"How'd you get caught in this stinkin' racket?" Fargo asked.

"I was passing through town and made the mistake of winning two hundred dollars in a poker game," the boy said.

"Penny struck up a conversation the next day," Fargo grunted.

Chuck Hapgood nodded. "I fell in love with her. I thought she was the most wonderful girl I ever met."

"I thought she was a damn cute little piece of ass," Fargo said. "We wound up the same way, though. Damn little bitch," he bit out.

"What's your name, mister?" Chuck Hapgood asked.

"Fargo," the big man said, his eyes narrowed in thought. "How many besides you?" he asked.

"Ten," Chuck Hapgood said.

"Where does he keep the others?" Fargo questioned.

"A prison barracks outside of town. I'm here because he's thinking of shipping me someplace, I heard," the boy said. "He makes money both ways, from those who have enough to pay him off and from the rest of us. The mines and logging camps pay him for supplying extra workers."

"They're going to have to find somebody else," Fargo growled. "I don't plan on staying around."

The younger man studied the big, black-haired man's handsome face, the jaw that could have been carved out of granite, the eyes that had become hard as blue agate. This was not a man for empty words, he decided, yet he shook his head ruefully. "I don't know what you're figuring, but running won't work. Others have run. They're brought in and the mayor trots out his files and takes them back in custody. He's got all the legal pieces in place. He's got everybody tied, marked, and packaged, and that goes for you, too," he said.

Fargo nodded. "That's why I don't plan to run, not the way others have," he said. "I'm just going to put an end to this stinkin' little racket."

The younger man stared back. "You sound awful sure of yourself, mister," he remarked.

"I don't know about awful sure, but I'm sure as hell awful mad, and that'll do," Fargo said as he settled down in a corner of the cell.

"We can take turns on the cot," the younger man offered.

"I'll be fine here," Fargo said and made himself as comfortable as possible. He wanted to let the fury seep through every part of his body as he slept without comfort until he was made of icy rage. When morning finally dawned he woke with the anger deep through him, determination a steel shawl. He was standing when the mayor and his three riflemen arrived, and he watched the stern, hawklike visage peer at him.

11

"Changed your mind?" Humphrey Wills asked. "Pay the three hundred and you'll only have six months to serve."

"Go to hell," Fargo said.

The mayor let an expression of disappointment slide across his face. "Stubbornness is a form of stupidity," he said.

"You're a form of slime," Fargo said.

The man's face grew dark. "Take him out. A week at hard labor ought to close his vicious mouth," he said. Fargo watched one rifleman open the cell and the second keep his gun trained on him while the third took a ball-and-chain from a closet and dragged it into the cell. Using a wide leg iron, he snapped the ball-and-chain around Fargo's left ankle, then stepped back and gestured with his rifle. Fargo started from the cell, dragging the heavy ball-and-chain across the floor. The three riflemen kept their guns steady on him, he noted. An unnecessary precaution, he grunted silently; the ball-and-chain very effectively made running out of the question.

Outside, they had an Owensboro seed-bed wagon fitted with two rows of wooden benches along the sides. He was placed in the wagon along with two of the riflemen while the third one climbed onto the driver's seat. The wagon rolled out of town and halted at the prison barracks about a quarter mile south, and ten men were marched out and into the wagon, each carrying their ball-and-chain. They noted Fargo's presence with short nods, each face heavy with resignation. The wagon drove south, toward the very edge of the Absaroka Range, and Fargo sat quietly and examined the lock on the ankle chain. The one rifleman had the key, the man who had put it onto his ankle. He wore a tan shirt and a yellow kerchief around his neck, Fargo noted. He sat back, closed his eyes, and felt the fury turned ice inside himself. They'd traveled perhaps an hour, he guessed, when the wagon

12

rolled to a halt and he opened his eyes to see the silver mine in front of him.

Four shafts, he saw quickly, set into the side of a low hill. A small operation, small, crude, and backbreaking, low shafts with little shoring at the entrance, the kind that quickly trapped stale air inside. He dropped from the tail of the wagon, holding the iron ball in his hand, and the other men followed. His eyes swept the mine again and saw a half-dozen other men moving in and out of the shafts, all unshackled. A fourth rifleman appeared to join the other three. Their job was plain—to keep watch on the jailbird workers. The rifleman with the yellow kerchief gestured to Fargo and two other shackled men. "You three, the first shaft there," he said and fell in line behind them as they started dragging themselves toward the nearest shaft. Three picks were standing against the wall of the shaft entranceway, and each man took a pick inside, Fargo drawing up last. They proceeded into the shaft, the tunnel deeper than he'd expected, and Fargo flicked a glance at the guard. The man stayed prudently behind. The other two workmen halted at a spot and began to dig for silver, using their picks on the stone and earth walls. Fargo found a spot and began to work alongside the others. He could barely stand up straight in the shaft as he struck his pick into the walls.

By midmorning he and the others had collected a fair pile of rock sand, earth, and stone from the walls. Two of the regular miners came in with a wheelbarrow and shovel and took the accumulated pile back outside. It would be put into rockers and sifted for signs of silver. "Back to work," the guard barked, and Fargo took up his pick and swung savagely at the wall of the shaft. He was perspiring heavily by midday, and his arms felt the strain of swinging the heavy pick upward in close quarters. Shortly after midday he and the other two men were taken outside, allowed fifteen minutes for water and a gruel-

13

like porridge. The regular mine workers stayed to themselves, he noted, and he wondered what stories they'd been given about the men who came in ball-and-chain. He heard the low, almost whispered words of one of the two men who had worked the morning beside him.

"I see you looking, friend. Forget it. You can't run. They only get you back, anyway. You run but you're a wanted man," the voice said. "Don't make it worse for yourself."

Fargo continued eating the porridge, answered without turning his head. "Thanks," he murmured. "Appreciate it."

The other man downed a cup of water, spit out words in between swallows. "But you're gonna try. I see it in you," he said.

"Not gonna try," Fargo murmured as he downed the last of the porridge. "Gonna break this fucking place wide open," he finished. The rifleman started toward him as he put the bowl and cup on the ground.

"Back inside," the man ordered. Fargo's quick glance saw the other prisoners being herded back into other shafts. He started forward into the shaft, saw the guard keeping back. The man had been well trained, he saw. He took no chances. Fargo took the pick up, began to chip away at the walls again, and felt his shoulder muscles groan. He had his plans thoroughly mapped out as the day neared its end. He heard someone blow a whistle outside. The other two men stopped working, started to trudge toward the entrance to the shaft with their picks. The guard followed them, paused to look back at Fargo.

"Move, mister," he barked. Fargo nodded, started to scrape his way forward, dragging the ball-and-chain behind him. It was only partly put on; his body was straining with aches. The guard glanced back at him, returned his gaze to the other two men. He had relaxed some, Fargo noted, aware that his prisoners were both exhausted and well shackled. The man's back was to him as he walked behind the other two men.

"Aaaagh, Jesus Christ," Fargo screamed. He fell to one knee. The guard whirled, rifle ready. Fargo, his head down, stayed on one knee, his face contorted with pain. "The pick," he gasped out. "I dropped the goddamn pick on my foot. Jesus, I think it's broken."

The guard came over and bent low. Fargo stayed on his knee, murmuring in groans of pain. His shackled leg would allow him no freedom of movement and no mistakes, he knew. Surprise and timing had to be perfect. "Get your hand back. Lemme look at your damn foot," the guard rasped.

Fargo drew his hand back, the guard's rifle only inches from his face. He straightened with the speed of a spring snapping, seized the rifle, and slammed the stock upward into the guard's jaw. The man staggered, his eyes glassy. Fargo twisted the rifle from the man's limp hands and brought it around in a short, vicious arc. The blow smashed into the man's throat, and Fargo felt the esophagus collapse. The figure crumpled in a heap at his feet. He reached down, pulled the keys from the man's pocket, and unlocked the leg iron, drew his ankle free. He saw the other two men, almost at the mouth of the cave, looking back with their mouths hanging open. "Walk on out. Act natural," Fargo said. "I'll be back for all of you come night."

"God almighty, mister," one man said in awe as he moved to the shaft entrance in the fast-fading light. Fargo followed, dropping to one knee just back of the mouth of the shaft, and looked past the two men dragging their way out. The other three riflemen were herding the rest of their prisoners into the seed-bed wagon. One turned as the two men came toward them.

"Ben?" he called, peered past them. Fargo watched the frown come over his face and he called to the other guards. "Watch them. I'm going to see what's holding up Ben," he said. He started toward the mine shaft. Fargo let him get halfway, then raised the rifle and fired. The guard seemed to suddenly do a little dance step and then pitch forward. Fargo's second shot came at once, and he saw the third guard fall, clutching at his shoulder. He fired again, two more shots, but the fourth guard had dived under the wagon, rolled to the other side. He came to his feet shooting, but the Trailsman had run, crouched low, darted into the thick mountain laurel. He kept running through the brush, dropped into a thick stand, and lay still, able to see the scene outside the mine shafts.

Others had come running, and the wounded guard regained his feet, one hand clutching his shoulder. Voices carried clearly to where he lay, but Fargo watched the dark closing in fast. "We'll get these men to the barracks first, then tell Wills," the fourth guard said. "He'll mount a search party. The bastard won't get far."

"I need a doc," the other guard mumbled as he climbed into the wagon, holding the rifle on the shackled men. The other man took the reins and rolled the wagon forward as the rest of the mine workers began to leave. They were all gone when night came to blanket the land, and Fargo rose to his feet. He began to beat a path upward, flattening the brush on both sides, making an obvious trail. The rifle had no more shells in it, and he dropped it along the trail. He went on again, laying the kind of trail a man running for his life would leave behind, a hurrying, headlong path.

He halted finally, moved to one side, and began to retrace steps, this time leaving not the faintest trail. When he reached the mine site he paused beside the guard lying lifeless on the ground, scooped up his rifle, and ran into another of the mine shafts. He dropped to one knee just back of the mouth of the shaft, the entranceway no more than a pitch-black hole now.

He settled down and waited. It wasn't a long wait before he heard the riders approaching. They came into view, and he counted eight with Humphrey Wills. They milled around the area just outside the mine shafts while four lighted torches. He watched the mayor form his posse into a semicircle and start into the hills, the men carrying the torches spaced in between the others. Fargo smiled when he heard their excited shouts as they found the trail and then the rifle. He saw the glow of their torches as they immediately set off on the trail, and he leaned back against a piece of wood shoring and relaxed. They were a determined lot, he decided, as half the night had gone by before they returned, straggling back with torches burned out.

"Sonofabitch won't get far. We'll nail him come daylight," he heard Humphrey Wills say. "Get Ben Elin's body out of that shaft and pick up the other feller," the mayor ordered. Fargo stayed unmoving as he watched the search party finally ride away with their lifeless burdens. The little smile edged his lips again. He had guessed right. They'd been certain their quarry had run up into the hills. If he had, they'd likely have flushed him out. They hadn't the imagination to think he'd hide under their noses. He rose, stepped from the shaft entrance, and started down the hillside. He broke into his long, loping, ground-eating trot. He was going to pay his father-in-law a surprise visit.

He crossed over a low hill that cut a mile from the road and saw the long, low, flat-roofed structure at the bottom of the slope. He moved down toward it, staying under the low-branched shadbush until he was close enough to make out the lone guard outside. The man seemed asleep in a chair leaned back against the door, a rifle across his lap. The shadbush came to an end some fifty feet from the barracks building, and Fargo paused, took another grip on the rifle in his hand, and started across the clear land. He ran, crouched over, silently on the balls of his feet. He'd almost reached the building when the guard came awake. The man blinked, was still focusing on the dark shape racing at him when the rifle butt crashed into his forehead. The chair skittered out from beneath him and he collapsed against the door.

Fargo picked up the guard's rifle, saw the door was held shut by an iron bolt from the outside. He pushed the bolt back and pulled the door open. He paused to bend down and take a ring of keys from the unconscious figure and hurried into the building. He saw a single, long room with two rows of cots, a lamp burning low at the far end. The men in the cots sat up, surprise in each face, a few daring hope. They were chained to the cots by leg irons, and he tossed the keys to the nearest man. "Unlock yourselves," he said. He stepped back, peered outside the barracks door as the men passed the keys down the line of cots, his eyes sweeping the night countryside. Nothing moved, certainly not the guard who lay half on his side, a tremendous lump forming over his brow. Fargo turned back to the men inside, saw they were standing, unchained.

"Take off. Get the hell away from here," Fargo said.

"What about all those warrants he'll have out on us?" one man asked. "I tried runnin' once. It didn't get me far."

"Try again," Fargo barked. "There'll be no warrants this time."

"Jesus, mister, we owe you," another man murmured, awe in his voice.

"He's got my horse someplace. Anybody know where?" Fargo asked.

"He's got a corral just this side of town. He keeps all the horses he takes there," a man answered.

Fargo nodded, turned to the door. "Good luck," he called back as he set off in the long, loping trot. The cor-

18

ral came into view soon, octagon-shaped, a shack beside it. No guards, he saw as he halted, swept the structure with piercing eyes. He spotted the Ovaro at once among a dozen or so horses inside the corral, broke into a trot, and saw the pinto's head come up, wide nostrils sniff the air. The horse let out a whinny, reared up on hind legs.

"Another minute, friend," Fargo called softly as he halted at the shack. The lock on the door was set into old, rotting wood that tore away easily. The inside of the shack was a single room crammed with riding gear, and he pushed the door open to let moonlight seep inside. He found his saddle and bridle in one corner and hurried outside to the corral. He was saddled up and riding toward Threadneedle in a matter of minutes, letting the pinto set his own pace. In the predawn hours, the town was dark and steeped in silence when he reached it. He slowed, moved carefully along the deserted main street. He made his way to the jail first, dismounted as he neared it, and left the pinto a half-dozen yards from the door.

A nightlamp burned low inside the front office, and he saw a man asleep inside, his feet up on the small desk. Fargo moved to the window, peered in at the sleeping figure. It was not anyone he'd seen before. Fargo rapped softly on the door. The man woke at once, swung his feet to the floor, and turned out to be a short, squat figure. He came to the door, stared out suspiciously. Fargo mouthed words, forming the words "Mayor" and "Wills" distinctly enough and slurring the rest. The man frowned. Fargo pointed impatiently to the locked door and formed the word "message" with his lips. The short figure inside stepped to the door and unlocked it, opened it a fraction, his hand on the gun in his holster.

"The mayor wants to see you," Fargo said. "He sent me to stay here till you get back."

"He wants me now?" the man growled. "In the middle of the night?"

Fargo shrugged helplessly and edged a step closer, saw the man let the door open a little farther. "Look, partner, I just follow orders," he said.

The man peered, pushed his head out farther. "Who're you?" he growled. "You weren't with the posse."

"No, I stay inside the house, kind of a bodyguard for the girl," Fargo answered.

The man stared at him, frowned, digested the reply. He let the door open a fraction more. Enough, Fargo decided. His blow was short, a quick uppercut that came up too fast for the eye to follow, all the strength of his biceps and forearm behind it. It caught the man under the chin, and the short figure staggered backward into the little front room. Fargo leaped after him, crossed a tremendous, looping left that spun the squat shape around as though it were a top and sent it crashing into the wall. The man slid unconscious to the floor, face still against the wall. Fargo took the gun from his holster and used it to smash the lock on the desk drawer. He drew his own Colt from the drawer, the gunbelt with it, and strapped it on. Only then did he turn to the cell where Chuck Hapgood stared at him, eyes wide with astonishment.

"I told you I'd be back," Fargo said as he found the cell keys and unlocked the barred door.

"I'll be dammed," the younger man breathed as he stepped out. Fargo dragged the guard into the cell and slammed the door shut. He handed Chuck the man's gun.

"Take it and get moving. There's a corral outside town where the horses are kept," Fargo said.

"You?" the younger man asked.

"Got some unfinished business, first," Fargo remarked.

"Much obliged to you for this," the younger man said. "Good luck to you."

Fargo nodded and let Hapgood disappear into the night before he walked from the jail to where he'd left the pinto. He had no trouble finding Mayor Humphrey Wills's house, having taken Penny there at least twice. But this time he circled around to the rear door. He closed his hand around the knob, turned slowly, and the door opened noiselessly. He let it hang ajar as he took his lariat from the pinto and then stepped inside the house. He followed the sound of snoring to the bedroom at the end of a hallway, the door to the room open. He entered, a noiseless ghost of a figure, approached the big, four-poster bed and the figure sleeping in it. The man's face was hawklike even in sleep, he observed as he took out his kerchief. He clapped it over the man's partly open mouth, pressing his teeth apart and pushing the cloth in as a gag.

Humphrey Wills woke at once, started to struggle. The touch of the cold gun barrel againt his temple halted his movements, and he stared up at the big man standing over him. He tried to talk, but the kerchief pushed into his mouth allowed only gurgling noises. Keeping the Colt against the man's temple, Fargo yanked him to a sitting position, wrapped the lariat around him, pinning his arms tight to his sides. He dropped the Colt back in its holster as he pulled the rope tighter and then bound the figure to the bedposts. He lighted the lamp beside the bed and took the kerchief from the man's mouth. The mayor sputtered out words instantly. "You must be crazy, coming back here," the man said.

"I took care of all your guards. There's nobody around to help you," Fargo said. The man glared back, and Fargo turned up the lamp on the bedside table. The kerosene-soaked wick flamed to light the room, and Fargo saw the doorway on the far wall. He opened the door and found a small study, a table, a wooden file cabinet, and two chairs filling the little room. A large cardboard

21

box of file folders jutted out from the file cabinet. Fargo leaned back to cast a glance at Humphrey Wills as the man struggled futilely to free himself. "I think I've found what I came for," Fargo said cheerfully.

The mayor stopped struggling, his eyes growing wide with apprehension. "You get away from my things, you hear me?" he shouted.

Fargo smiled, walked into the small study, and pulled the file box from the cabinet. He carried it into the bedroom and set it on the table. The mayor's face had grown blood-red with frustrated rage, he saw. "Keep your hands off those things," the man shouted. Fargo smiled as he began to riffle through the file folders.

"Look at all this," he commented. "Marriage certificates, witness signatures and all. And the preacher's signature, too. All alphabetically arranged." He continued to poke through the folders until he halted, pulled one out. He smiled as he read aloud. "Fargo . . . Skye Fargo, married to Miss Penny Wills," he said. "Look at this, my very own marriage certificate." He lifted the cover from the lamp and held the edge of the file folder to the flame. It caught and quickly began to consume itself. When it was blazing high he dropped it into the box with the other folders.

"Goddamn you," Humphrey Wills rasped, tried to get free, and cursed in pain as he dug the ropes into his wrists. "You won't get away with this, you bastard," the man shouted.

"I sort of think I will," Fargo said calmly as the entire box of folders began to go up in flames. "Mighty nice little fire, isn't it?" He smiled cheerfully.

"No! No, you sonofabitch," Humphrey Wills shouted as he threw himself about in an effort to tear free. The big bed shook, but he remained bound to it. The file box burned high, engulfed in flame in moments, collapsing into ashes on the table. The mayor's throat made strangled little sounds as Fargo went to the bureau and got the porcelain pitcher of water, poured it onto the smoldering ashes until there was nothing left but a black, soggy mound. He put the pitcher back in its place and smiled at Humphrey Wills.

"No more files, no more victims. It's called the end of a rotten, stinking racket," he said.

"I'll get you for this," the man rasped.

Fargo was about to answer when Penny's voice cut in as she called from the top of the stairway outside the bedroom. "Daddy, you all right? I heard you shouting. Are you having one of your nightmares again?" she called.

The big Colt snapped into Fargo's hand, and he put the barrel against the man's temple. "You sure are, Daddy," he whispered. "Worse than any before. Tell her to come down."

The man hesitated, and Fargo drew the hammer back on the big Colt. "Penny, come down," Humphrey Wills called, his voice a hoarse croak. Fargo listened to the girl's footsteps as she came down the stairs, holstered the gun as she came into the room. She wore a frilly pink nightgown and looked fragile, fresh, and innocent. When she saw him her cupid's-bow mouth dropped open.

"I missed out on my wedding night," Fargo said. "I came back to make it up to you."

He watched the anger, instantly followed by alarm, swim into her face. He stepped toward her, eyes cold as blue agate, and she started to back away. "Now, you just wait," she began.

"Wait, hell," he hissed, and his hand shot out, seized the front of the frilly nightgown, and yanked her forward. The thin material tore in his grasp, and two rose-fleshed, pink-tipped breasts tumbled out. She tried to twist away, but he caught her wrist, spun her around, and held her with her arm behind her. "You're the damn

23

heart of it," he growled. "Without you, little Miss Pussy-Bait, Daddy could never make it work."

He heard Humphrey Wills shout, "Leave her be, Fargo. I'll do right by you."

"She'll do right by me," Fargo tossed back as he marched Penny from the room and pushed her up the stairs.

"I'll kill you," he heard the man roar.

"Go to hell," Fargo called back as he pushed Penny into her room, released her wrist, and flung her halfway across the bed against one wall. He went after her as she whirled on the bed, aimed a kick at his testicles. Expecting the move, he was ready to dodge aside, and he seized her by the torn nightgown. She flung herself to one side, and the rest of the garment tore away. Her pink-fleshed body fell onto the bed, rounded, curvaceous, a little belly and a modest curly triangle. He fell onto her, and she tried to get her knee up but he knocked her leg aside, and she lay on the bed, the convex pubic mound waiting in front of him. Anger and desire mixed together inside him, and the eager maleness rose, demanded liberty, now as much a weapon as a gift. Her innocent-appearing face, the kewpie-doll lips, were suddenly infuriating symbols of deceit and treachery. He found the warm, dark portal that tried to twist away from him, and he thrust into it roughly. Her scream of pain was no act, and he drew back, frowned down at her.

"Goddamn," he growled. "All that pussy-waving and you're a damn virgin."

Her answer was to bring her knee up to try for his groin again. He half-turned, knocked her leg to the side, and opened the dark portal again. "Rotten little bitch," he hissed, pushed into her again, but this time he slid in less roughly.

"No . . . aaaiiii . . . oh, goddamn, oh, goddamn," Penny's little kewpie-doll lips screamed. "Oh, oh, oh,

God." Fargo slid deeper, pulled back, slid forward again. "Bastard," she hissed. "Oh . . . oh, Jesus." He saw fury and pain in her face as she tried to fight away pleasure. "No, no . . . oh, oh, oh . . . oh, my God," she gasped out as he moved back and forth inside her, faster, slower, faster again. Her nails dug into his back, and he saw her mouth fall open, the pink-tipped breasts lift, fall back, pleasure beyond denying now. "Ah . . . ah, ah . . . ah, please . . . no, please . . . oh, no . . . oh, yes, oh, Jesus." The words fell from her lips as she arched her neck, and he quickened his pace. He felt her pelvis start to lift, and he rammed deep as she cried out. "Oh, no, no . . . iiii . . . iiieeeee," the scream rising as he let the engorging moment engulf her. "No . . . No, bastard . . . oh, God . . ." she cried out, epithets and enjoyment tumbling over each other until he pulled roughly from her and he saw her curved little body flinch at the sudden denial.

He rose, looked down at her limp, panting form, her eyes glazed with shock and satisfaction, anger and ecstasy. He laughed as he saw the anger slowly pushing all else aside. "Sorry, the honeymoon goes with the marriage. They're both over," he said.

"Bastard," she whispered. He laughed again as he strode from the room. She had enjoyed it, despite her anger, and that was the only thing he was sorry about. He bounded down the stairs and paused at the door to the bedroom. Humphrey Wills, his body twisted as he still tried to free himself, stared out at him, the hawk face dark with rage.

"I'll be talking about you to the first federal marshal I meet," Fargo said. "Try starting up again and you'll be behind bars."

"I'll get you for this, Fargo. I'll get you if it's the last thing I do," the man shouted.

"It will be," Fargo said and walked away. He left by the rear door, his own anger satisfied.

The dawn was just beginning to break over the distant mountains of the wild Absaroka Range, and he headed the pinto toward their towering crags. He wanted a lone and wild place without the smell of greed and deceit, a place to relax with only the wild pureness of nature surrounding him. He rode until he was into the mountains and the sun had climbed high in the sky. His body knew the ache of exhaustion, but he pressed on higher into the mountain fastness. The Absaroka Range lay at the southerly end of the great Rockies, a wild and uncharted range of its own known best to a few mountain men and the Arapaho. When the weariness refused to be pushed aside any longer, he found a place under a spread of red ash at the top of a long, valleylike slope of rich bluegrass. He unsaddled the pinto and let the horse run free to forage at will. The pinto would roam the valleylike slope, he knew, grazing, enjoying the feel of freedom, yet he'd not go beyond hearing. Fargo laid his bedroll out, sank down on it, and slept soundly as the dusk began to creep slowly down the high peaks.

3

The morning was growing full when he woke, stretched, enjoyed the sweet smell of honeysuckle growing nearby. He used his canteen to wash and, dressed, he stepped out from the red ash and let his eyes sweep the valleylike slope of the land. He gave a sharp whistle, then another, and waited for the pinto to appear. When the horse failed to come into sight he whistled again, his eyes scanning the far side of the slope. Nothing moved but a flight of red-winged blackbirds. He whistled again, louder and longer this time, but his gaze found no glistening black-and-white Ovaro. The frown crept across his forehead, and he stepped farther out onto the slope of rich blue-grass, searched the treeline again that formed on the opposite ridge. He whistled once more, waited, and the uneasiness stabbed at him.

Something was wrong. He knew his horse. The Ovaro would respond at his call. Unless he had wandered too far, and Fargo frowned at the thought. It was unlikely. He might wander, but he'd return with the dawn if not before. Something was wrong, he repeated silently. He cast a glance back at the saddle and bedroll under the red ash, adjusted his gunbelt, and moved out across the green slope. He spotted the pinto's tracks quickly enough, still fresh in the soft grass, followed their trail down the slope. It became a criss-crossing path, as the pinto had run wide in a free-form pattern. He followed the evenly spaced prints where the horse had walked, the deep-dug-in hoofmarks where he'd run in freedom, and the areas of chewed grass where he'd halted to graze.

The prints roamed back and forth down the valleylike terrain and up the other side, and Fargo halted, whistled sharply again. But there was no response, and his lips turned in on each other. Something was very definitely wrong. The Ovaro wouldn't have run off. Unless a wild mare in heat had come by, he frowned. That was a possibility, he realized. There were others less pleasant. Cornered by a cougar was one. Twisting an ankle and being run down by a wolf pack was another. The horse might have panicked at his plight, run blindly. Damn, Fargo swore inwardly as his eyes returned to the marks in the grass. He followed the Ovaro's prints again, up to the top of the other slope this time, to a line of alders. The horse had still been running free and fully in control of his own pathways. Fargo halted to press his hand into the hoofprints in the grass. Still damp, the grass still smoothed. Not more than a few hours old. The Ovaro had still been all right as dawn came.

Fargo moved after the prints again until he suddenly dropped to one knee, his eyes scanning the ground. His mouth drew tight. No cougar, no wolf pack, and no mare in heat. The ground was marked with deep imprints of shod horses, riders on horseback. He rose, went forward, saw the line of the Ovaro's tracks move away, going into a gallop as the hoofprints grew farther apart. He also saw the other horses give chase, spread out, and come together again halfway down the ridge. He ran, halted, saw the cuts in the soil made by hooves digging in deep, hind legs pulling backward, as when the rider has roped a steer. But it was no steer. It had been his Ovaro they had lassoed. Fargo followed the prints as they moved down the far side of the slope, pausing often to study the marks, which told him as much as the printed words in a book told ordinary men.

They'd roped his horse, four riders, pulled him with them down the other side of the slope. Fargo moved forward, halted again, dropped to one knee to study the indentations in the soil. The Ovaro had bucked, reared, fought. But the marks went on, the Ovaro's prints now shortened and close together. They had hobbled him to keep him from acting up. Fargo grunted. They'd have damn slow going with a hobbled horse. He rose and began to trot, moving forward into the long, wolflike loping gait that let him devour ground at a rhythmic, steady pace. They had but a few hours' start, their trail fresh, easy to pick up. He went on down the slope to the flat land below, cast a quick glance behind him to mark his path. But even traveling with a hobbled animal, they were still on horseback. He wouldn't catch up with them quickly. He ran, half-crouched, moving after the tracks that materialized in front of him.

The sun moved across the sky, into the afternoon, while below, the lone figure moved with the effortless grace of a prowling mountain lion. The long, loping stride let him run with only infrequent pauses to rest, the motion in rhythm with the roll of the land. It was late afternoon when he drew in sight of the four horsemen. He spotted the Ovaro at once and hurried his pace. The men had halted at a small stream, and he moved toward them, closing the distance quickly. Two of the men were drinking from the stream, the other two standing by. The tallest of the four, a man with a tall crown on his hat and a yellow kerchief around his neck, saw him first. He spoke to the others, who turned at once as Fargo trotted up to them. He saw each man rest a hand on his holster, and he kept his own arms hanging down loosely as he came to a halt. His lake-blue eyes swept the quartet at once, typical saddle dusters, leathered faces with suspicious eyes. The tallest one with the tall-crowned hat had a hooked nose and a thin mouth.

"Where'd you come from, mister?" he asked, not hiding the surprise in his voice.

"Been following you," Fargo said.

The man frowned, glanced at the others. One, a shaggy-haired man, stepped closer. "Following us?" he asked. "On foot?"

Fargo nodded, gestured toward the Ovaro. "You've got my horse," he said.

The hooked-nose man's face deepened. "You're crazy, partner. We roped that critter this morning. He was running wild," he said.

"I let him run free during the night," Fargo said.

"No way. He's one of the mustangs that run these hills," the man said.

"A mustang with shoes?" Fargo questioned. "Or didn't you notice?" he added, the question its own accusation. Even a greenhorn would have been quick to spot the shoes. He saw the man's eyes harden.

"I guess I didn't," the man said. "And just because he's got shoes doesn't make him your horse, mister."

"That's right, don't pay no mind to this bum, Coley," the shaggy-haired one cut in, stepping forward. He peered hard at the big, black-haired man in front of him. "Get out of here, mister," he said. Fargo's eyes, ice-floe cold now, stared back without blinking, and the other man looked away quickly. Fargo let his glance sweep the quartet. Each man had a hand on his gun, ready to blast him into the ground. He grunted silently. Too many, too spread out. He could get two, maybe three, but not four, not the way they were positioned and waiting. He took a step backward, his ice-floe eyes moving from one man to the other.

"He's my horse. I'm going to get him back," he said quietly.

"You'll get a bullet up your gut if you come around here again," the man called Coley answered. Fargo turned and loped away, not looking back. He heard one of the men utter a harsh guffaw, kept moving on until he was out of sight over a low hill. He edged to his left, continued to go on, confident that one had followed to the hilltop to make certain he was leaving. He loped on alongside a bank of hackberry, gave himself enough time and distance, and suddenly the lone figure had melted into the trees as a shadow melts into darkness. Fargo halted, dropped to one knee and rested a few brief moments, then turned and, staying in the tree cover, began to retrace his steps.

The four men had left when he reached the stream, but he followed their tracks with ease, caught up to them as dusk began to settle over the land. They had made camp in a small glade beside the hackberries and hawthorns. They had been heading south, he noted, and he saw they'd tied the Ovaro to the trunk of a sapling. He crept closer with the darkness and heard their voices raised in argument. The man named Coley stood apart from the others, his voice that of command. "I said we'll take turns standing guard," Fargo heard him insist.

"It's crazy. He ain't comin' back. He's scared shitless," the shaggy-haired one growled.

"Eddie's right," another man agreed.

"Hell he is," Coley snapped. "That big bastard followed us all damn day to get his horse. He'll try again. Didn't you see his eyes?"

"He's on his way to get himself a new horse by now," the shaggy-haired one said.

"You know the boss will pay us a bonus for that Ovaro. He'll be real excited to get him. You want to lose a bonus or some sleep?" Coley pressed. Fargo saw his words hit home as the others fell into a reluctant silence. "Three-hour shifts," Coley said. "Eddie and Sam, the first one." Fargo stayed motionless, watching, as the shaggy-haired man and one of the others moved to take up guard positions, one near his Ovaro, the other a short distance away. Coley and the other man bedded down at once, and Fargo waited until the two sleepers fell into rhythmic, heavy breathing. He continued to stay motionless, a silent, shadowed form in the trees.

"Screw this," he heard the shaggy-haired one say. "I'm gonna get me some shut-eye. You can stay awake if you want to be dumb," the man muttered. Fargo watched him slide down against a tree trunk near the Ovaro. The other man stayed on his feet, but leaned his back against another tree, his body relaxing, shoulders drooping. The still, dark shape in the forest moved forward, soundless steps, closer to the man standing against the tree.

Fargo took the heavy Colt from its holster, held it by the long barrel. The figure against the tree let his eyes half close as Fargo came up closer. He was unaware of anything until the butt of the big Colt smashed down onto the back of his head, and then awareness was his but a flickering moment, a sharp burst of pain and then the relief of unconsciousness. Fargo caught the man's arm as he started to collapse, eased him to the ground, but the man's boot hit against a stone to send it skittering across the ground. Shit, Fargo swore silently.

The shaggy-haired one came awake at once. "Sam?" he called in a half-whisper. Fargo stayed on one knee beside the unconscious figure, watched the other man pull himself to his feet and frown into the darkness. "Sam?" he called again in a tight whisper. Fargo swore inside himself again. A damn loose stone and everything came apart. The shaggy-haired one had started toward him, he saw. He came up from one knee in a diving, hurtling leap. The man saw the figure materialize, tried to dodge aside, but Fargo smashed the butt of the Colt into his jaw. He heard the crack of bone as the shaggy hair seemed to leap upward as if it were suddenly unattached. The figure gave a gasped cry of pain before toppling to the ground, and Fargo, peering past the quivering bulk on the ground, saw the other two men sit up. The fourth man rolled, came up with his gun, and his first shot was a wild, too-quick explosion. Fargo dropped low, spun the Colt in his hand, and found the trigger with his forefinger. His shot caught the man as he started to stand.

"Aaaagh, Jesus," the man cried out in pain as he staggered backward, the gun falling from his fingers as he clutched at his shoulder. The man called Coley was rolling like a pinwheel, Fargo saw, came up half behind a tree, and Fargo dived away as he caught the flash of gunfire. The bullet whistled over his head, followed by two more as Coley fired from the protection of the tree. Fargo lay flat, flung himself into a quick roll, crashed into the nearby brush as another two shots came too close. He rolled again, into deeper cover, halted, and pulled himself into a half-crouch. Coley had taken the moment to reload, Fargo knew, and his eyes swept the little glade. "Christ, my shoulder . . . Jesus, Coley, I'm bleedin' bad," Fargo heard the fourth man cry out. "Coley, you hear me?" the man said, his voice rising in pain and alarm. "I'm bleedin' bad."

Fargo grunted silently. Coley was too smart to answer and give away his position. Fargo strained his ears, but the fourth man's groaning and crawling covered any other sound. Fargo's mouth grew tight as another groan rose, and he saw the shaggy-haired figure quiver, stir. There was no chance of picking up Coley's movements now. Fargo swore inwardly, and he backed, lowered himself almost flat in the brush. He waited, unmoving, silent, heard the man with the cracked jawbone murmuring pain-filled curses through a face swollen out of shape. Coley was taking time, being very careful, timing his every step with a groan or curse of pain, but suddenly Fargo glimpsed the dark shape moving between two tree trunks. He raised his arm slowly, took his hat off, and laid it on the ground beside him. His eyes were riveted on the tree trunk as one of the other men let out an angry half-groan, half-curse. The dark shape moved at once, darted behind another tree. Fargo brought the Colt up, aimed through the curtain of brush in front of him, and waited for another groan. It came a few minutes later, mixed with a curse, and Fargo saw the dark shape move out from behind the tree, half in a crouch, pausing to peer toward him. The big Colt barked once, a sharp, shattering sound in the dark woods, and the shadowed form seemed to leap backward. Fargo heard the man's gargled gasp as the bullet all but split his chestbone. He rose as the figure collapsed to the ground.

The voice called out from the glade. "Jesus, Coley?" it asked.

Coley didn't answer. Coley wouldn't ever answer anyone again. Fargo turned, moved forward, and came out in the glade. The shaggy-haired one sat against a tree with his misshapen jaw and stared up in pain at the big, black-haired man. The wounded one rested on the ground, one hand clutched to his shoulder, his arm and shirt a stream of red. Fargo's eyes went to the first man he'd smashed with the Colt. The figure lay face down, slowly crawling, still only partly conscious. The two men able to look up stared at him with disbelief still in their eyes.

"Jesus," the wounded one gasped out. "Who are you, mister?"

34

"Fargo," the Trailsman answered, his voice ice. "I know you'll remember it. You're the lucky ones. You're still alive. You might remember that, too, the next time you think about horse-stealing."

He swept the three again with a quick glance and backed from the glade, stepped to where the Ovaro was tied. He cut the hobbles from the horse with his knife and pulled himself onto the warm, bare back of the Ovaro, received a whinny of greeting. He rode away unhurriedly. The remaining trio would groan and limp their way back to wherever they came from. Maybe they'd learned a lesson, he mused, and felt the cynicism rise up inside him. He'd not bet much money on it. He pointed the Ovaro back the long way he'd come.

It was morning when he reached the place where he'd left the saddle, and he bedded down in the shade, slept until the noon sun was in the sky. When he finished washing and had dressed, he turned the Ovaro deeper into the Absaroka Range, drawn by the lone wildness. The sweet-sharp scent of balsam fir and red pine beckoned, and he climbed higher into the mountains to find large areas of rolling hillsides covered with evergreens with the land flattening out at the bottom of each slope to form a small high-country plateau lush with violet wood sorrel, doveweed, and the red-berried nightshade. He watched towhees furiously raking leaves, catbirds swooping in their characteristic flight, and a golden eagle in its soaring beauty. He wandered idly, enjoying the untamed beauty of the mountains, glimpsed a black-footed ferret, and saw a pair of martens scurry through the woods. The gnawed bark on a stand of black maple told him that elk herds were plentiful, and he paused when he picked up the signs of a wolf pack.

He dismounted, studied the wolf marks, guessed there were at least ten in the pack, the trail hardly a day old. They'd be a formidable group to encounter, he noted grimly. He swung back onto the pinto and cut away from the wolf tracks to continue his relaxed, idle wanderings. It was midafternoon and he'd just topped a rise covered with the tall stalks of orange mullein when he saw the horse just below, a striking buff-colored mustang with a yellow mane. The horse stood still, and Fargo halted, let his eyes move over the high arch of neck, the strong short-coupled body, the strong forehead planes of the head. No ordinary mustang, he commented silently, and suddenly the horse turned its head to him, catching his scent. The mustang began to move away, and Fargo saw the horse limp, a painful limp, as he seemed unable to put weight on his left foreleg.

Fargo watched the horse move, the limp almost disabling, and he edged the Ovaro slowly down the slope toward the wild steed. The buff-colored form tried to move faster and had to slow at once. Fargo moved his pinto in a half-circle, edging closer to the mustang, and he thought about the wolf-pack tracks. The lamed mustang would be a perfect mark for the pack, unable to run or to fight. He loosened his lariat and moved the pinto closer. If he could get a close look at the lame leg he might be able to help, Fargo thought. Or he could take the mustang in tow, keep him close enough to be safe. The mustang was far too beautiful a horse to become wolf fodder. Fargo neared the wild horse, saw the animal's attempts to get away become more desperate as, aware of his helplessness, he grew agitated.

"Easy, now, easy . . . it's all right," Fargo said in a low, soothing tone. It would have little effect on the wild horse, he knew, but it did succeed in bringing the mustang's ears up, caused him to pause in his limping gait. Fargo sent the pinto into an explosion of speed and flung the lariat at the same instant. He saw it drop over the mustang's neck, and he began to tighten in at once. The mustang's lameness gave him little chance to fight the lariat, and Fargo slid from the saddle to slowly move along the lariat toward the mustang. The horse tossed its yellow mane, tried to pull away, but the lame leg sapped its strength at once. Fargo moved forward along the lariat, taking it very slowly. He was halfway to the horse when the shot exploded in the hollow. He heard the sharp sound and felt the searing pain in his temple all at one instant, and then there was nothing, only the total blackness of unconsciousness.

4

The world returned with pain, raw, angry burning, his temple on fire. He heard his breath in a hoarse sound as he pulled his eyes open and a gray curtain slowly began to lift. Remembering came back as the grayness lifted, the shot, the searing pain in his temple. He blinked, shook his head to clear away the last of the grayness despite the pain. Objects began to take shape, trees, sky, clouds. He was on his back, and he felt the roughness of rope around his wrists, realized his arms were bound behind him. He pushed himself to a sitting position and felt the emptiness of the holster at his side. He breathed a curse as the figure stepped into view in front of him, came into focus, became a young woman.

Tall, she stood very straight and seemed even taller than she was. She held the rifle in one hand at her side. Fargo's eyes took in medium-brown hair, shoulder-length, framing a face that could have been rawboned were it not for the slender nose, the high cheekbones that gave her striking planes and a strong, clean line of cheeks. He saw a wide mouth, set firmly now, well-formed lips, and eyes the gray-green color of sage. An arresting face, no sweet prettiness in it but a strong, almost wild handsomeness. His glance took in the rest of her, a slender figure just avoiding boniness, legs that revealed only their length in the riding skirt, and a buckskin vest that hid the shape of her breasts.

"Who the hell are you?" he growled at her.

"You know who I am," she said.

"The hell I do, and you ought to be more careful with that damn rifle. You could've killed me," Fargo said.

"I could have. I'm a crack shot," she said, and the simple matter-of-fact way of her told him to believe her words.

Fargo pushed down with his bound hands, got to his feet. "You tie me up like this, dammit?" he barked, and she nodded, the sage-color eyes taking in the intense, handsome, chiseled face of the big man before her. "Well, untie me, dammit," Fargo ordered.

"No way," she said calmly.

"You crazy?" he threw at her. "What the hell did you shoot me for?"

Her lips turned a shade thinner, and the sage-color eyes darkened. "You know what for. You were going to take that mustang," she said. "You bastards will take every rotten opportunity."

"Honey, I don't know what you're talking about," Fargo said.

"Don't you call me honey," she snapped, "and don't lie to me. You're one of Jack Egan's, and I know it."

"Honey, you don't know shit," Fargo said. "Who's Jack Egan?"

He saw the sage-color eyes shoot fire. "You're a lot bolder than most, aren't you?" she said.

"Being shot and tied makes me right irritable," Fargo said. "And I don't know Jack Egan."

She uttered a short, harsh laugh. "You're one of his pack, all of you murdering, horse-thieving slime," she said. "Only one of Jack Egan's men would grab the chance to rope a lame horse."

"I roped him because he's going to be wolf bait if he's not in hand," Fargo flung back at her.

She frowned into space, her lips thinning. "I know—that's why I was after him. I'd best get moving before he gets too far away," she said, almost as if to herself. He watched as she turned and strode to a long-legged chestnut with a white patch on his forechest. She threw the Colt on the ground as she swung onto the horse. "I figure you'll be able to work those ropes loose in three or four hours, if you know how to do it," she said.

"Dammit, you're making one big mistake," Fargo shouted.

She wheeled the chestnut, paused to look back at him, her high-planed attractiveness severe and unsmiling. "There's only one reason I didn't put a bullet through you, and you wouldn't understand it," she said.

"Try me," Fargo shot back.

"Your horse," she said very seriously.

"My horse?" Fargo frowned.

"A man rides a horse like that can't be all bad," she said and touched the chestnut on the rump. The steed broke into a fast trot at once.

"Come back here, dammit," Fargo shouted, but she pushed the trot into a gallop, no glancing back, hair swinging from side to side. She rode beautifully, he noted, back very straight, head held high. She made a sharp turn, and he watched her disappear into the trees, a very real kind of wild beauty in her as she became one with the horse. He cursed softly as the hoofbeats faded from earshot in the trees and he began to try to slip his wrists out of the ropes. He felt the bonds give, then hold tight against a double knot. He dropped to his knees as he began to move his wrists back and forth to try to loosen the ropes further. He pulled, twisted, turned for almost an hour until he halted to rest, arm and wrist muscles throbbing. She'd done a damn good job of tying him, he swore silently when he tried again. He halted the second time, convinced the ropes couldn't be loosened. He rose, scanned the trees, his eyes moving past white ash, hackberry, hawthorn, halting as he saw the sugar maple. He walked quickly toward the trees with its coarse, grainy, warty bark, put his back to the wood, and began to rub the wrist ropes up and down the trunk.

He felt the ropes move over the coarse-grained bark, catch on tiny bumps. He had to rub carefully to avoid shredding the skin on his wrists against the bark, and he had to halt to rest frequently. He cursed each time he saw the dusk laying a lavender mantle across the mountains. Unable to see his wrists, he could guess his progress by the touch of the bits of rope that dropped onto his hands. He tried to hurry only to yelp in pain as he scraped his flesh against the coarse bark. Forcing himself to work slowly, doggedly, he continued to rub the ropes against the warty bark as night crept over the land. He made a mental note of where the Colt lay on the grass before night dropped its stygian cape. It was sudden when it happened, the wrist ropes shredding apart, and he yanked at his wrists, felt them come free. He brought his arms in front of him, stretched cramped muscles, and began to rub circulation back into his hands. It would take three or so hours to work loose, she had said, and he cursed her for being so right.

He retrieved the Colt and called the pinto. The horse came at once, and Fargo used the water from his canteen to wipe the dried blood from his temple and along the side of his face. Damn, he'd not just ride off, Fargo swore as he swung into the saddle, not after being shot, tied, and accused of being part of a pack of murdering, horse-thieving slime. He'd been framed once within the past week. It wasn't going to happen twice. He'd get some answers from that wildly beautiful, rifle-toting girl. He headed the pinto into the trees where he'd watched her disappear. He slowed at once, a half-moon filtering only a glimmer of light through the foliage, not enough to pick up tracks. He moved the pinto through the shadowy shapes of the forest, emerged on the other side of the timber stand to see a narrow strip of clear land and another stand of timber directly across it. The moonlight, unfiltered through thick foliage here, afforded enough light for him to see, and he slowly moved the pinto up and down along the edge of the opposite stand of timber. He pulled to a halt as he found what he sought, the thin branches snapped off where she'd plunged into the timber, riding hard.

He followed, not hurrying, the forest again quickly closing out most of the moonlight. She'd had at least three hours to catch up to the lame mustang, more than enough time, he reflected. But if she'd roped the mustang and stayed with him he'd have slowed her down plenty. She'd not be all that far ahead now. If, he grunted. She could have changed direction in the timber, decided she couldn't help the mustang and gone off on her own. Yet it wasn't the kind of thing he saw her doing, not with the real concern for the horse he'd felt from her. He pushed on perhaps another half hour, aware that he'd not be able to pick up a trail until the morning light, and he had just reined up at the edge of a little glade when he heard the shot. Unmistakably a rifle, it came from directly ahead of him, perhaps a quarter of a mile, he guessed. Two more shots resounded, and he sent the pinto into a fast trot, weaving his way through the trees.

Another shot resounded, and he shifted directions some ten degrees to his right. Two more shots exploded, closer, and he heard that special scream of a horse in fear. He continued to push through the woods as fast as he dared ride in the darkness, and another two shots shots exploded the night and then he heard the snarls, deep-throated growlings, and the rifle barked again. He was almost at a gallop when he reached the scene, a spot where the trees thinned to let in more moonlight. He saw the gray-brown shapes first, a swift-moving circle of darting, snarling attackers. The girl came into sight, crouched behind a log, her own chestnut and the lame mustang behind her, both horses pulling at their tethers in fear. She was too close to the horses and wasting shots, but he'd no time to teach her now as he saw the circling shapes begin to close in.

Fargo saw the girl turn as he raced to a halt, surprise on her face. He drew the big Sharps rifle from the saddle case as he leaped to the ground, sent a quick shot in the direction of a gray shape coming toward the horses from behind. The shot missed but the wolf dodged back, the attack broken off. Fargo dropped down beside the girl for a moment and saw the surprise still in her eyes as she glanced at him. "I'll take the other side of the horses," he said, rising, backing away, and darting around behind the lame mustang. He was just in time to see the dark-gray form hurtling toward the horses, a second one close behind. He fired, heard the first wolf yelp in pain. It rolled on the ground but regained its feet and raced into the trees with the other one. He heard the girl fire, three quick shots, as his eyes watched the moving shapes in the trees, passing across his sights too quickly. They were constantly moving, circling, darting forward, then vanishing in the trees, nothing aimless in their planned, clever movements. They were a pack, their hunting techniques perfectly synchronized out of instinct and intelligence. He waited, finger on the trigger of the big Sharps.

Suddenly he heard the girl fire a volley of shots, then her scream rising in the darkness. He raced around the horses to see the trio of wolves attacking from two sides. The girl, trying to defend against all three, succeeded in bringing down none. Fargo dropped to one knee, took aim at a black shape hurtling through the air, and saw his shot hit squarely on target. The wolf half-turned in midair to drop dead, inches away from the girl. The other two wolves were leaping past her, heading for the horses. Fargo's shot ended one's leap just as it began, and the other wolf swerved directions, ran off into the trees. Fargo whirled, fired at two more gray-black shapes, and the girl followed his fire with two shots of her own. One wolf, grazed, half-turned, ran off, and the other swerved away.

Fargo whirled as he heard the snarl on the other side of the horses, saw the chestnut rear up and kick out and cry in pain. Fargo raced around the two horses in time to see the wolf beside the animals, leaping up to attack again, too close to the chestnut to risk a direct shot. He fired two shots past the wolf and saw the gray form drop low, half-turn, race away to vanish into the trees. The chestnut's upper leg streamed blood, and Fargo stepped to the wound for a quick glance just as the girl came into sight, backing around the horses toward him, rifle held high. Her eyes filled with alarm and concern as she saw the chestnut's wound. "A slash . . . not really deep," Fargo said and suddenly became aware of the silence, total, absolute, a silence that seemed its own kind of noise.

"They've gone," the girl whispered, her eyes round with apprehension. "Just disappeared." Fargo, in a half-crouch, swept the trees surrounding them, and nothing moved. "They were just there, suddenly, and now they've just gone," the girl breathed, awe in her voice.

"That's their way," Fargo said, his eyes still scanning the trees. "But they'll be back," he said and saw her take a deep breath, stare at him for a long moment. "We didn't hurt them enough for them to stay away. I want to be someplace better than this when they come again."

"I was heading for my cabin when they attacked. I've a wire-fenced corral there," she said. "It's another hour away."

"We can try," Fargo said grimly.

She started for the chestnut, paused to look at him. "I owe you," she said. "But that doesn't mean my taking you home with me."

"You'll never make it alone with the gimp-legged mustang," Fargo told her. "I might not, either. They've a taste for horsemeat tonight. Together, we stand a chance."

She thought for a moment, the moonlight touching the planes of her face to give her a stark beauty. "Yes, I suppose you're right on that," she said. Her eyes turned to him, studying his face. "I was right on one thing. A man rides an Ovaro like yours can't be all bad," she said.

"That's the only thing you're right about," he said. She turned away and went to the mustang, and he saw the rope halter she'd thrown around the wild horse. He watched as she put her hands on the lame mustang's shoulder, held them there, gently moved her palms up along the horse's neck, and he caught the sound of her murmuring softly to the animal. He felt the tiny frown touch his brow as the wild horse remained quiet and she slowly tugged at the rope halter. The mustang began to limp after her as, still murmuring softly to him, she pulled herself onto the chestnut. She had that touch, that very special magic inside her, the quality that let her reach out to wild things, and Fargo grunted silently. It was something he could understand better than most. Whoever she was, or whatever she carried inside her, she was different from most. He swung onto his horse and fell in behind the lame mustang.

"I'll ride back a ways," he said, and she nodded and began to move forward through the trees, climbing upward. Fargo rode silently a dozen feet behind her, his eyes scanning the dark forest, but he knew he'd not see anything until they were ready to be seen. The land grew more steep, and she continued upward, their progress painfully slow because of the lame mustang. He'd guessed almost an hour had gone by and they continued to climb. "I'd be a damn sight happier if you'd move out of this timber," he muttered.

"Soon," she said over her shoulder. But it was another half hour before he saw the trees begin to thin and let in more moonlight. Suddenly he felt the pinto's gait tighten into short, prancing steps, and he saw the horse's ears twitch nervously.

"Rein up," he said softly. "Get your rifle ready."

She halted but had to pull back twice on the chestnut, he noted as he moved up to her. Alarm in her eyes, she glanced past him into the trees. "I don't see anything," she whispered.

"I don't either," he said. "But look at the horses. They know." He slide from the saddle as she continued to peer into the trees for another minute. When she swung to the ground he had tethered his horse with enough slack rope for him to kick backward and come down with his forelegs if necessary. He helped her tie the lame mustang short and gave the chestnut enough room to maneuver. He pointed to a spot a few feet on. "You get over there. You'll be back far enough to cover both sides of the horses from the front. I'll do the same from the rear," he said.

She nodded and walked to where he'd pointed, settled onto one knee. "They'll come in and out, first. Don't waste bullets. Wait till one really attacks," he said.

"How will I know that?" she questioned.

"They usually make test runs coming in at an angle. When they attack for real they come barreling in straight and fast, so watch how they're coming in at you before

46

you fire," he said. She nodded, and he drew back to take up a position beside an elm that gave him a clear view of both sides and a wide angle of fire. He rested on one knee, the big Sharps held across his leg. They hadn't made it to her wire-fenced corral. Luck wasn't riding with them, he silently commented. He hardly breathed, his ears straining, and suddenly he picked up the sound, faint, soft, padded footsteps. He peered through the trees and the gray-black shapes materialized as if out of the air, moving to circle the horses. He caught the flash of yellow-green eyes, saw the big form at the head of the pack complete the circle, and now the others darted forward, staying low to the ground, making the circle smaller.

The pack leader suddenly swerved, came straight at the horses, and Fargo raised the rifle as the wolf paused, seemed to survey the scene with one quick, green-yellow glance, and then darted into the shadows. He lowered the rifle, raised it again at once as he saw two dark forms break into a full run at the horses, coming from his side. He fired, the first shot hitting the animal nearest him, and he saw the wolf flip sideways in midair, hit the ground to lie still. He swerved the rifle, fired again at the second wolf as it continued to streak for the horses. His shot slammed into the racing shape at the back of the skull, and the wolf, momentum carrying it forward, sprawled forward, almost at the rear of the horses. Fargo saw the Ovaro's hind legs strike out, and the wolf's carcass sailed through the air not unlike a furry rag.

He heard the girl's rifle bark, saw her bring down another attacker. The pack had decided to attack in force. Fargo saw another gray shape hurtling forward, and the girl's shot brought it down. He fired a shot at two darting shapes that swerved away, then he saw the chestnut rear into the air, exploding with the sudden strength of panic. The tether snapped, the branch tearing away, and Fargo saw the horse bolt. Instantly, a half-dozen gray shapes streaked after him.

"No, stop . . . Blaze, no!" he heard the girl scream and saw her leap to her feet to start to race after the horse. The chestnut skidded to a halt between two trees, tried to turn, and the wolves were at him at once, coming in from all sides. "No, Blaze, here . . . over here!" the girl screamed as she ran. Her attention was focused only on her horse as she ran toward the animal, firing wildly as she did. She never saw the gray-brown shape coming at her from the side. Fargo brought his rifle up to fire, but she was in the way, and he cursed as he dropped the rifle, flung himself forward in a flying tackle. He hit her at the knees just as she raced past him and she went down with him. He felt the wolf's paws hit the top of his head as the animal hurtled through the air. The wolf landed on the ground but a few feet away, spun around, and charged, yellow eyes and gleaming fangs, a terrible guttural roar from within the powerful chest. Fargo yanked the Colt from its holster, managed to bring it up and fire point-blank at the snarling, fanged jaws coming at him. He emptied the gun and flung himself sideways, pulling the girl with him. The wolf, jaws now dripping blood, fell almost on top of him, the great form twitching, then lying still.

Fargo sat up, felt his breath come in a long gasp, and he saw the girl spring to her feet, eyes seeking the chestnut. She retrieved her rifle, started to run toward the horse, then halted and peered into the trees, and he was aware that once again they were surrounded by silence. His eyes circled the trees, and nothing moved, but this time the ground was dotted with lifeless gray shapes. The chestnut had halted a dozen yards away, and Fargo watched the girl run to him, examine his wounds, and finally lead him back.

"They got in a half-dozen slashes this time, but none

are real deep," she said. "He can make it to the cabin."

"He's lucky," Fargo said.

Her eyes traveled around the circle of trees, fear in her face. "Will they came at us again?" she asked.

"Not likely tonight," Fargo said. "Wolves can be vengeful, and we didn't get the pack leader. But they've been hurt. They'll lick their wounds and probably move on come morning."

She turned, took the mustang's rope halter and the chestnut's reins. "I'll walk him. It's not that far," she said. "He'll bleed less without the pressure on his legs carrying a rider."

"So he will," Fargo agreed, waited as she turned and started to slowly walk forward along ground that began to level. She understood horses, he observed again, with the head and the heart, only understanding was too weak a word. It was something more, a communication, a special bond that no earthbound reasons could explain, a kind of touching given to some from another time beyond memory. He followed, leading the pinto, and he guessed they'd gone another quarter hour when the timberland came to an end and he followed her out onto a high plain that stretched a dim silver under the moon. He saw the cabin some fifty yards farther, a lamp burning inside with a welcoming square of amber light. The small corral reached out from one side of the cabin, wire overlying the fencing. Under her hands, the mustang went in without protest, and she led the chestnut to one corner, roped him short to a fencepost. As Fargo unsaddled his horse and led him into the corral, she disappeared into the cabin to return in minutes with a heavy jar filled with a cream-white ointment. Using only her hands, she began to apply the ointment to the horse's slashed flesh.

"Oil of mountain balm, mugwort, cocklebur, and yarrow, best salve for wounds I've ever found," she said. She paused to glance at him. "You want to wash up, there's a well and bucket back of the cabin," she said.

He nodded and left her tending to the horse. Walking around the cabin, he saw the well pump handle and the oak bucket near it, took off his shirt, gunbelt and trousers. He pumped fresh water into the bucket and washed off trail grime, dried himself with his shirt. He pulled his trousers back on but nothing else and stepped around to the front of the cabin. She was inside when he entered, and he saw her eyes take in the hard-muscled, beautifully balanced body that combined power and grace. The cabin was a large single room with a fireplace, a bedstead in one corner, two Texas chairs with rawhide seats and a quilt rug on the floor. A puncheon table occupied another corner of the room, and one wall was hung with harnesses and rope halters. The girl reached behind a woodpile and brought out a jug, pulled the stopper from it, and brought the mouth of the jug to her lips. She took in a long draft and held the jug out to him. He drank from it and felt the kick of cold hard cider, drew another long drink, and handed the jug back to her. He felt the tiredness clouding over him, as though the cider had unleashed a floodgate of weariness.

"You live up here all by yourself?" he asked as he put his gunbelt on the table.

"Here, and other places," she said, and he caught the wariness in her voice.

"Where are we?" Fargo asked.

"In the Beartooth Mountains of the Absaroka Range," she told him. Instinctively, his left hand moved to touch the big half-moon scar on his right forearm. Her eyes followed the motion, questioned silently.

"She-grizzly," he murmured.

"You were lucky. Most men tangle with a grizzly don't live to tell about it," she said. She offered the jug again, and he shook his head. She put it behind a woodpile inside the cabin. He watched her shed the buckskin vest, but the heavy cotton shirt beneath it still kept her breasts undefined. Fargo saw the sage-color eyes appraise him. "I owe you again," she said matter-of-factly. "You're a strange one, different from the rest of them."

"Because I'm not one of them, whoever they are," Fargo said sharply.

A rueful half-smile touched her wide mouth. "You going to keep pretending?" she asked.

"You going to keep being so goddamn suspicious?" Fargo shot back.

The half-smile lingered on her lips. "You were close enough to help because you'd been following me," she said. "You going to lie about that, too?"

"No, you're right. I was following you," he conceded.

"To get to that mustang," she said.

"No, to get to you," he flared, and realized at once how the words had sounded. "Not that way," he added quickly.

"A slip of the tongue?" she returned, and he saw the smug satisfaction in her face. "But you'll not be having me or the mustang," she said. She turned to the bedstead and reached under the pillow. When her hand came out it was holding a big Whitneyville Walker Colt, one of the old models with the nine-inch barrel.

"Goddamn, you're made of suspicion," Fargo flared. "You don't believe anybody or anything, do you?"

"Not often and not now," she said.

"You owe me. You said it yourself," Fargo reminded her.

"I do," she agreed.

"You've a damn funny way of showing it, honey," he growled.

"I'm giving you and your horse a safe place to sleep the night," she said. "Now, I'll admit that's little enough for your saving my neck, but it'll have to do for now. I just can't take any chances, can't and won't."

"That I'm one of this Jack Egan's men?"

"That's right," she said.

"Goddamn, I told you I don't know the man," Fargo threw back.

"You told me, but that's all words, that's all you have, words that don't fit your following and chasing," she returned with cool certainty. He studied her high-planed face. Too much suspicion, too much distrust, to be swept away by words, even reasonable, logical ones, he saw.

"You're a hard-nosed case, aren't you?" he muttered angrily.

She shrugged. "I'm what I have to be," she said.

He eyed the big old Whitneyville. "You can't hold that on me and sleep," he said.

"The cabin's yours. I'm sleeping right outside the door in my bedroll. You can't say that's not being hospitable," she said with grim irony. She picked up his gunbelt and backed toward the door. "Don't try coming outside. I'll be right by the door and I'll wake up shooting and I don't want that," she said.

"I wouldn't want that, either," he agreed.

She paused at the door. "Sleep well," she said, and there was no bite in her words. He nodded, and she closed the door after her. He felt the tiredness dig at him, and he undressed and lay down on the bedstead, two thick blankets serving as a mattress. He didn't fit without drawing his knees up, and he lay awake in the dark as his thoughts lingered on the strange young woman outside the door. The wildness of her was not made just of outside angers. It was a part of her, deep and running free inside her, a very special quality that set her apart from most. Something with this man Egan obsessed her. She wasn't afraid, but she was fearful. There was a difference, but he knew one thing for certain. Come morning he'd

52

find out what this strange, wild girl was all about. He closed his eyes and sleep came at once, a heavy, exhausted sleep, and he did not wake until the morning sun rose high enough to come in through the cabin's single window.

He rose, pulled on trousers, and stepped to the window to see the girl walking toward the cabin, drying her hair with a towel. Little beads of water still glistened on her face as she lowered the towel. She seemed to almost shine with the freshness of the morning columbine, her hair loose, a cotton blouse tucked in tight at the waist to outline modest breasts that curved saucily upward at the tips. He watched as she halted, surveyed the hillside. She fitted into these mountains, her beauty a fierce, proud beauty, he decided. He saw her start to move toward the corral, and he left the window to pull the door open and step outside. She halted, her glance taking in his bare-chested, powerful figure, and he caught the flash of appreciation in the sage-green eyes.

"Morning," he said and received a nod.

"There's a stream just the other side of those mountain laurel bushes if you've a mind to bathe," she said. "I'll put coffee on."

He nodded and walked to his saddlebag, took hard soap and a towel. He noticed that the big Whitneyville Walker was tucked into the top of her skirt. He made his way through the mountain laurel to find a wide stream, plenty deep enough for bathing. The water, cold yet warmed just enough by the sun, imparted a welcome tingling to his skin as he soaped himself down, dried himself partly with the towel, and let the sun do the rest. Pulling on trousers again, he started back to the cabin, and the smell of fresh coffee marked an invisible path. When he emerged on the other side of the bushes, he halted in surprise to see the chestnut trotting freely, moving without visible pain, his own horse grazing nearby, and the girl in the corral with the mustang. Her back was to him as she held up the mustang's left forefoot, and Fargo felt the frown stab at his brow as he watched the mustang stand perfectly still. Finally, the girl straightened and Fargo watched the mustang put his foot down, back from her, execute a half circle, follow with a full circle, only the hint of a limp in his gait. The girl pushed the corral gate open further and the mustang bounded free, yellow mane blowing against his buff-colored hide as he raced down the slope, continued on till he was out of sight.

Fargo turned to watch the girl come out of the small corral. She extended her palm, and he saw the short, sharply pointed piece of branch in her hand. "It was deep in the frog," she said. "The more he stepped on it, the deeper it went."

"And he just let you dig it out," Fargo said, not hiding the respect in his voice. "You've a way with wild things. You understand them and they feel it. That makes you special."

"Compliments?" she asked, one brow arching.

"Truth," he returned.

She went into the cabin, and he followed. Two tin cups of hot coffee were on the table and she took one, pushed the other toward him. She sat down across the table from him as he drank slowly, savoring the strong, bracing flavor and inhaling the aroma.

"How'd you come to work for a man like Jack Egan?" she asked.

Fargo shrugged away answering and let his eyes take in the harsh yet almost classic beauty of her. Her upturned breasts pressed lightly against the white blouse as she drew deeply from the tin cup. "What happens now?" Fargo asked.

"You go your way and I'll still be beholden to you. I'm not the forgetting kind," she said.

"I'm damn sure of that," Fargo commented dryly.

"Maybe someday, sometime, I'll be able to repay you for the good things you did last night," she said. "Maybe you'll quit riding for that scum of a man."

"Maybe," Fargo said. "I just go on off, just like that."

"Not quite. I'll take you down into the low hills. You'll wear a blindfold," she said.

"What the hell for?" he bristled.

"Egan hasn't found the way up here. I brought you up in the dark and I'll take you back that way," she said.

"He'll find you sooner or later if he keeps looking," Fargo suggested.

"Maybe, but it'll take time. It won't be with you showing him the way," she said, and the bitterness was in her voice at once.

Fargo let his eyes touch the big Whitneyville Colt in her skirt. "Do I get my gun back?" he asked.

"When we part company," she said.

"Guess there's not much I can do about it," he sighed. "Can I finish my coffee, first?"

"Yes, of course," she said, and he took another sip of the black brew, swirled it in the tin cup, seemed to relax in acceptance of the situation. He saw her watching him, a hint of reluctance in her eyes. "I'm sorry it has to be this way," she offered.

He allowed a rueful smile and a quick shrug. "You do what you have to do," he said.

She nodded gravely, but he saw her relax at his apparent understanding and acceptance. He swirled the coffee in the cup. It was barely warm now, and he flicked a quick glance at the girl, saw her stare into space for a moment. He waited a second more, saw that her hand was far enough from the gun at her waist, tightened his fingers and wrist, and struck. His wrist snapped the tin cup upward, the stream of coffee sailing through the air. She let out a gasp of surprise and dismay as the coffee hit her full in the face. Her eyes blinked shut in a reflex action, but her hand reached for the heavy revolver at her waist. Fargo's arm snapped out, his big fingers closing around the butt of the gun as he yanked it away from her. He flung it into a far corner of the room as her eyes came open and she swung at him, tried to rake her nails across his face.

"Bastard. Sonofabitch bastard," she hissed. He pulled away from the raking swipe of her nails, seized her elbow and forearm and twisted, and she yelped in pain as he spun her around.

"Now, we're going to talk," he said. He felt her leg move, but the sharp pain took him by surprise as she brought her bootheel down along the side of his ankle. "Ow, goddamn," he muttered, and his grip on her arm relaxed for an instant. It was enough for her to tear away. She spun, swept one of the tin cups from the table, and flung it at him. He just managed to duck in time to avoid taking the cup in the face, glanced up to see the kick coming at his groin, and twisted sideways. The kick landed on his hard-muscled thigh, and the momentum of the blow threw her off-balance. He snapped an arm out, caught her by the wrist as she tried to duck away, yanked her around to face him. But once again he had to pull away as she clawed out with both hands, fingernails aimed at his eyes.

"I'll kill you, you rotten bastard," she screamed as she missed with her downward swipe. He came in from the side, caught her shoulder, and spun her around. His foot landed hard against her rear, and she fell sprawling forward across the cabin to land on the floor.

He started toward her, expected her to turn, but she got to one knee and half dived, half ran through the open door. "Damn," he swore as he raced after her. He caught up to her outside as she streaked toward his saddlebag, hands outstretched to close on the rifle. He tackled her,

56

fell forward with her, got an arm around her waist, and had to let go as she brought her rump up hard under his jaw.

Half crying and half cursing in wild rage, she wriggled forward and dove for the rifle, but he caught her ankle and yanked and she slid backward with a yelp of pain. He pressed one big hand into the small of her back, pinning her to the ground, as he brought his other hand down hard across her rear. "Ow! You rotten bastard," she cried out. He brought his hand down again and then again, hard blows, her rear rounder than he would have suspected, and she screamed and cursed and tried to wriggle free but he kept her pinned face down on the ground. He administered two more stinging blows and flipped her over, fell forward half atop her, pinning her arms to the ground.

"I'll get you, you goddamn lying bastard," she hissed as she tried to lift herself free, twist away, get her knees up. But his body held her immobile as he looked down at her eyes blazing dark fury. She blew a lock of hair from her face, tried to turn her head to sink teeth into his wrist. He half-lifted her, banged her down on the ground, and she let out a gasp of pain.

"Cut it out, damn you," he roared, banging her head on the ground again. "You're going to listen to me or I'll fan your ass so hard you won't be able to sit a saddle for a month." He felt the soft-hard touch of her under him as she tried to twist free again, and he banged her head once more against the ground.

"Bastard," she murmured as she glowered up at him, but he felt the push go out of her body.

"I'm not one of this Jack Egan's men," Fargo growled at her, met the fury of her eyes with his own anger. "You're just so full of suspicion you can't believe anything else of anybody."

"More words," she spat out.

"Damn little wildcat," he snapped. "I'll give you more than words." He pushed backward from her, releasing her arms, sprang to his feet "Get up. Maybe I should toss you in that stream and cool down that wild temper," he said. She pushed herself up on her elbows and he saw her measure the distance to the rifle. He took a step backward. "Go on, you can probably get to it," he said. She stared at him, and he saw the confusion creep into her sage-green eyes. "If I were who you keep saying I am I'd have you hog-tied, or worse, maybe, and be on my way after that mustang," Fargo said.

She glowered from beneath the frown that had come to crease her brow. "Maybe," she murmured.

"Maybe?" Fargo shook his head. "Jesus, you're a hard case." He stepped to her, reached out and yanked her to her feet with no attempt to be gentle. She brushed her hair back, her eyes peering deep into him as she put one hand behind her.

"I hurt, damn you," she muttered.

"You could hurt a lot more," he said. "Now, are you ready to talk?" Her silence as a kind of agreement. "Start with your name," he said.

"Thorpe. Prudence Thorpe," she said.

"Prudence?" Fargo almost laughed. "That sure as hell is the wrong name for you."

"It is not," she bristled.

"It's as wrong as a name can be. Prudence is for quiet, polite girls, back-porch girls that sew samplers, not a half-wild creature living in the mountains."

"Fit or not, it's my name," she snapped with a mixture of pride and defensiveness. "What do they call you?"

"Fargo . . . Skye Fargo. Some call me the Trailsman," he answered.

Her brows lifted a fraction. "That explains your picking up my trail in the damn dark," she muttered. She peered at him, and he saw her breasts push against the blouse as she drew a deep breath. "Maybe I did have you all wrong. I'm sorry for that," she said. "But you'd do the same in my place," she added quickly.

"What is your place? What the hell are you all about?" Fargo threw at her. He saw the anger leap in her eyes at once, and she whirled, strode to the chestnut, spun to face him.

"You want to know what I'm all about? All right, dammit, I'll show you," she flung at him. She turned and leaped onto the chestnut, using his mane as grip and reins. He saw the angry challenge her eyes flung at him as she wheeled the chestnut and raced away. Fargo was at the pinto in two long strides and vaulted onto the horse, used his knees to wheel the pinto in a tight circle. He took after Prudence Thorpe, clinging to the Ovaro's back with easy grace. He caught sight of the girl, followed as she raced along a slope and swerved sharply to cut upward through a narrow passage lined with cottonwoods on both sides. The passage climbed steeply, turned, leveled out, and suddenly emerged onto a mountain plateau. Prudence pulled the chestnut to a halt, watched him as he rode up to her and his eyes swept the plateau. The herd of mustangs were spread across half the small plateau, and Fargo halted, his eyes sweeping the awesome, breathtaking sight.

The mustangs looked up at him, some moving, ears standing straight, the others content to watch warily. Suddenly the pack moved to the left, almost as one, not unlike the way a field of wheat ripples in the wind. Fargo saw dark bays and roans, grays and whites, buffs and reds. A tall stallion, a shining deep brown, came forward a half-dozen yards, watched the two intruders at the edge of the plateau, then moved back into the rest of the herd.

"Beautiful," Fargo murmured.

"Beautiful and free," Prudence said as she slid from

the chestnut. Fargo eased himself from the Ovaro, saw her eyes search the wild horses. "He's not here," she said.

"Who?" Fargo asked.

"The leader. He's jet black and he moves as though he were a shadow. I call him the Wild Shadow," she said. "When you ride him you don't feel there's a horse under you. It feels as though you're riding on air."

"When you ride him?" Fargo frowned. "You've ridden a wild stallion?"

"Yes," she said matter-of-factly. "More than once. We're friends, he and I . . . of sorts. I ask nothing and he knows it."

Fargo's stare was made of astonishment and admiration, and he saw the girl's face shine with a wild beauty, her long-legged, lean body almost an echo of the proud, beautiful mustangs. "Yesterday and tomorrow are out there in front of you," she said. "Mustangs, but no ordinary mustangs." She moved the chestnut back to a line of brush and lowered herself to the ground, sitting cross-legged, showing nicely tanned, shapely legs as she did. Her eyes moved back and forth across the wild horses, and Fargo sat down beside her, watched a filly kick her heels and bound away in playful exuberance. "No offense, but you most likely don't know what you're seeing," Prudence said. "Most cowhands know very little about horses except how to work them."

Fargo let a small, tight smile touch his lips as he scanned the pack of wild horses. "I'm not most cowhands," he said as his eyes moved over the mustangs to take in the elegance of their heads, the fine lines of the slightly dish-faced profile on most of them. He studied their heads, the flared nostrils, the small, neat ears, and the slight bulge over the forehead which extended to below the eyes.

"The Arabian is damn strong in them, judging by the

pronounced *jibbah* on most of them," he said, using the Arabic word for the forehead bulge.

He saw the surprise in her eyes as she cast an appraising glance at him. "You do know your horses, don't you?" she said. "You're right, except that the Arabian is more than strong in them. It's almost pure."

"Pure?" he questioned. "You've something more than their good looks to say that?"

She nodded. "Arabians have one fewer vertebra than other horses. It's their genetic badge. These mustangs are short one vertebra. I've examined those who've died of injuries or age."

Fargo frowned at her. "How do you account for a herd of Arabian mustangs here?" he asked.

"There are others up in these mountains," she said. "Of course, some have bred with Indian ponies and other wild stock, but they've stayed basically pure. When I first came on them I went back and did a lot of research. These horses are the descendants of the horses the Spanish conquistadores brought to the Americas. They used the Spanish barbs that were bred by the Moors in North Africa."

"The Spanish barb was a variety of the Arabian," Fargo said.

"Exactly, and the Spanish conquistadores went a lot farther into the west than overrunning the Aztecs. Vasquez de Coronado marched as far north as Kansas and as far west as the Grand Canyon. De Soto discovered the Mississippi. So the horses they lost along the way were able to spread out through the West."

"And they lost a lot of horses, I'd guess," Fargo commented.

"Many to the Indians," she nodded, "and a lot that just ran off. But the Indians lost plenty, also. The Indians don't geld their stallions, and so a lot of the finest Arabian stallions they'd stolen simply ran off and became wild horses. Either way, for a long time there was no other blood for them to mix with. The wild Arabians mated with each other to remain as pure as if a breeding farm had been directing things. It was only centuries later that other stock came on the scene to mingle with the wild Arabians. These were horses brought west by colonists, explorers, and soldiers. Finally there was a lot of mixing, and today, most mustangs are a mixture of all kinds of bloodlines."

"But not these," Fargo said, nodding to the herd.

"Not these," Prudence echoed. "They stayed a pure pocket here in the Beartooth Mountains. The Arabian qualities of strength and intelligence were a heritage which let them survive. The Arabs bred their horses to survive in harsh places. These pure, gorgeous animals are living proof of that."

Fargo's eyes roamed across the herd again, and he lingered on the magnificence of their lines, the proud stature and mercurial spirit that was the mark of the Arabian. "They're something special," he said. "But all this doesn't answer my question. Where do you fit in? And this Jack Egan?"

He saw Prudence Thorpe's eyes cloud at once, her jaw grow firm. "Jack Egan's a rotten bastard, selfish, stupid, and greedy, and without an ounce of honesty or principle," she said. "He's a horse dealer, and he's been wanting these horses ever since he learned they were up here."

"And you're against that," Fargo said.

"You're damn right," she snapped.

"Why? A good breeder could maintain the purity of the herd, establish a program of selective breeding," Fargo said.

"Only that's not Jack Egan. He's out to round up all the ones he can catch and destroy the ones he can't rope. That'll give him control of all these Arabians. Once he has them he'll breed to anything anywhere or just sell them off to anybody for the best dollar he can get. That's the cut of the man. He doesn't care about horses, just dollars. Jack Egan doesn't care about anything but himself."

"That the only reason you want to stop him?" Fargo asked.

"Isn't that enough?" she threw back sharply.

"It's enough. Now how about answering my question?" he pressed.

Her lips tightened for a moment. "All right, they're free and wild and they deserve to stay that way. They breed enough outcross mares this way to improve the ordinary mustang strains. For hundreds of years they've been free and wild, and that's the way they ought to stay. Maybe, someday, that'll be impossible. But that'll be something for another time, and I most likely won't be around then. But this is now and I'm here and that rotten bastard isn't going to destroy these free and beautiful animals."

She halted, drew a deep breath, and he saw tiny points appear for an instant against the blouse and watched her eyes shine as she gazed out to the herd. "This Jack Egan, he knows you're out to stop him, I take it," Fargo said.

"He knows," she said with flat grimness.

"I recall you said he and his men were a murdering pack. That just angry talk?" Fargo questioned.

"No. I hired a young fellow, Jeff Bridger, to help me. Less than a week later he was killed and left on my doorstep," Prudence answered.

"I thought you said no one knew the way up here to your cabin," Fargo frowned.

"They left him at my pa's place down at the foot of the mountains. It's my place now since my pa died," she said. Fargo saw her lips part and her eyes suddenly grow bright, and her voice dropped to a whisper. "He's here," she breathed.

"Egan?" Fargo frowned, turned to follow her gaze.

"No, the Wild Shadow," she whispered, and Fargo's eyes moved up to a ledge of flat rock and he felt his own breath draw in sharply. The jet-black horse looked down from the flat piece of rock, suddenly there, as though an invisible giant hand had dropped him in place. The stallion tossed his head and the black mane streamed to one side, and Fargo's gaze stayed on the magnificent horse, taking in the proud, alert carriage, the glistening ebony coat, the color itself unusual for an Arabian. The horse switched his tail, stepped a few paces back, and leaped with effortless grace, into a narrow path that headed down from the ledge, almost obscured by rocks and shrubs, to emerge onto the mountain plateau. The herd parted for him as he ran through their ranks, circled and halted in front of the others, reared on his hind legs, came down and pranced, and the horses nearby moved back in a gesture of respect and submission. Fargo saw the stallion turn his head imperiously, stare across to where Prudence gazed at him. He moved, started toward her, went into an easy trot, and Prudence walked forward to meet him.

Fargo watched the black horse halt and Prudence put her hands on his neck, keep them there for a long moment, then move her palms across the long arched crest and up to the black mane. Holding the mane, she swung herself onto the stallion's back, and the horse spun, raced away instantly, galloping into the herd, moving in and out among the other horses like a black wraith. Prudence lay low over the mustang's back, one with the racing horse, as though she were glued to him. The stallion made a wide circle through the herd and returned almost to the spot where she'd swung onto his back. He halted and pawed the ground, and Prudence slid to the grass, moved her hand along the side of his strong neck. She turned from the horse and started back to where Fargo waited, met his gaze with turbulence in the sage-green eyes. She halted in front of the big black-haired man, her breath shallow, tiny dots of red touching her high-planed cheekbones.

"He's gone now," she breathed, and Fargo lifted his eyes to gaze over her shoulder. The stallion had vanished. His eyes scanned the herd but could find no proud jet form.

"Yes, he's gone," he nodded.

"The Wild Shadow," Prudence murmured and walked past him to the chestnut.

Fargo walked with her, his gaze narrowed at her as he halted beside the pinto. "I'm impressed," he said. "Twice, now, if that's what you'd a mind to do."

"It wasn't for that," she said simply. "Come on, I'll take you back to the cabin."

Fargo allowed a wry smile. "I can find my way back," he said.

Her eyes were made of disbelief, and he pulled himself onto the pinto and tossed her a short laugh as he rode on. He heard her following as he retraced steps without hesitation. When he finally pulled up in front of the cabin, she came up behind him, her eyes on him as he slid from the pinto. "My turn to be impressed," she said as she dismounted.

"I may have run into some of Jack Egan's men," he told her and recounted the story of the four who'd tried to make off with his horse.

"You did," she grimaced when he finished. "And now you've listened to me and you've seen something few men have. You've anything to say on it, Trailsman?" she thrust.

"Your heart's right. Your head's wrong," he said.

"What's that mean?" she frowned.

"It means you can't fight off Egan and a passel of his men all by yourself," he said.

"I could use help," she admitted quickly, and he saw the question form in her eyes.

"No, thanks," he said.

"Afraid?" she thrust.

"No, just not a damn fool," he returned.

"It takes damn fools to do the important things," she answered, her chin lifting. "If you care enough, odds don't matter. I thought showing you those wild, free, magnificent creatures might make you understand. I guess I was wrong about you."

She was spearing with words, but it was more than just that, he realized. She hurt, felt so strongly, so totally, that she'd no room for compromises and no patience with those who couldn't care as she did. "I understand, more than you know," he said gently.

She refused to be mollified and gave a derisive snort. "More, but not enough, it seems," she snapped.

"Damn, you're full of nettles," he said.

"Why not?" she flung back, and he had no answer.

"I'll try to help. I'll go see this Jack Egan. Maybe I can get him to listen to me," Fargo offered.

"Forget it," she dismissed.

"I've seen folks listen to reason," Fargo countered. "Where is his spread? A horse dealer has to have a fair-size spread."

She hesitated, then answered, her voice full of crossness. "South, when you reach the low plains," she muttered.

"I'll come back. I'll tell you what he said," Fargo promised.

"I don't give a damn what he says. And you won't come back. He'll see to that, one way or another," she said.

"Meaning what?" Fargo asked.

"He'll persuade you to forget about me. He's a smooth talker. Or he'll kill you if he figures you might help me," she said.

"He won't be doing either. I'll come back," Fargo promised.

"Don't bother," she snapped. "I told you, I don't give a damn what Jack Egan has to say and I won't believe it anyway." She picked up her saddle and began to strap it on the chestnut, paused to turn to him, her eyes mirroring a mixture of pride and defensiveness. "Thanks again for last night. I still owe you," she said.

He nodded and met her appraising gaze. "Where are you going now?" he asked.

"I've things to check, plans to get ready," she answered. "Egan will find his way up here sooner or later. I'm no fool. I know that. I want to be ready when he stumbles his way up here."

"How will you be ready?" he asked.

"Ready to fight or to run or both," she said. "I know just about his every move, and I'll be ready when he comes."

"How do you know his every move?" Fargo asked.

"I get information," she said cryptically and offered nothing more. Fargo knew it would be a waste of breath to press her. "I thought maybe you'd be the kind to stay and help me," she said.

"You thought wrong," he grunted.

"You said you understood, about the mustangs. I think you do. Are you afraid?" she pushed at him.

"Now it's your time to know better," he said.

She half shrugged. "Then you don't understand," she grumbled.

"I understand, but I've my own trails to follow. I can't take on every damn cause," he said.

"It's not for me, dammit. It's for the right to be wild, for those magnificent animals," she flared.

"I'll talk to this Jack Egan," he offered again.

She climbed onto the chestnut, turned the horse in a tight circle, and glared down at the big man. "Don't bother coming back," she snapped. She brought her hand down sharply on the horse's rump, and the animal shot forward. Fargo watched her streak away, brown hair streaming out behind her, the rush of wind flattening the blouse against her breasts, a beauty made of wild defiance and wild love.

She vanished into a line of timber, and Fargo turned to his own horse and began to saddle the Ovaro. Finally he slowly rode down the mountainside. He made his way through the timber, using all his skills to find the trail back and mark it in his mind for future use. It was after noon when he reached the low plains and headed the pinto southward.

5

He'd ridden less than an hour south when the ranch-house came into view, a stable alongside it and two corrals spreading out on either side of the house, neat, white-painted fences enclosing each. He saw the name EGAN hung over a fencepost as he rode to the house, and ten or twelve horses corralled, a half-dozen men working with them. Another four men were near the ranchhouse as he rode up and halted at the hitching post outside the front door. One question that had clung in his mind was answered as he recognized two of the men, the shaggy-haired one and the other who still sported a swollen, misshapen jaw. He saw the shaggy-haired one set down a bucket he'd been carrying, his jaw dropping open in surprise as he saw the big, black-haired man. Fargo watched him bolt into the house through a side entrance.

Fargo dismounted unhurriedly, draped the Ovaro's reins over the hitching rail, and cast another glance at the spread. He let his eyes move past the stable, noted the doors were closed, let his glance linger on six saddles sitting atop a fence rail near the stable. He could smell the saddle soap fresh on them from where he stood. He started for the door of the ranchhouse, had just reached it when it opened and a man stepped into the doorway.

"Looking for somebody?" the man asked.

"Jack Egan," Fargo answered.

"You found him," the man said, and Fargo felt the surprise pushing at him. Jack Egan was considerably younger than he'd expected, and a lot more handsome. Fargo's eyes took in a chiseled face, even features, a straight nose, pale-blue eyes, a strong face with light-brown, almost sandy hair. A slight dip at the corners of his mouth hinted at arrogance, but only one thing that marred the handsomeness of his face, a long, red, ugly scar that ran diagonally away from the center of his forehead, just below the hairline, across the left side of his head to his temple. "You've brass coming here, I'll give you that much, mister," Jack Egan said.

"Didn't know they were your men till I saw them just now," Fargo said.

Jack Egan took a moment before accepting the reply. "You did a job on them. Coley was a good man," he said.

"He was stealing my horse. I could've killed all four of them," Fargo said.

Jack Egan took in the reply silently. He was tall, Fargo took note, with muscle under a good frame tightly covered by a gray shirt. "Fargo, they said you called yourself," Egan said, and the Trailsman nodded. Egan lifted his head, a hint of imperiousness coming into his handsome face. "What do you want here?" he asked.

"Come to talk to you," Fargo said.

"About what?" Jack Egan questioned with a touch of impatience.

"About Prudence Thorpe and those mustangs up in the Beartooth Mountains," Fargo said.

Jack Egan's eyes widened at once, and Fargo saw his jaw grow tight. "You come here to talk about Prudence

Thorpe? You're either crazy or you don't know much," the man said.

Fargo shrugged. "Maybe some of both."

Jack Egan's brow creased. "You see those mustangs?" he asked, and Fargo nodded. "Her, too?" he added, and the Trailsman nodded again. The man continued to study him. "You find your way there by yourself or by luck?" he asked.

"Neither," Fargo said. "Tell me what I don't know."

"I'll tell you there's nothing to talk about," the man said.

"Seems to me there is," Fargo said calmly. "Seems maybe with a little reasonableness you and Prudence Thorpe could work something out about those Arabians."

He saw Jack Egan's pale-blue eyes take on a chilling frostiness. "Not with that crazy, wild woman," Egan said, his voice growing harsh. "I'm going to wipe out every one of those goddamn horses."

Fargo frowned at the man. "That doesn't make much sense," he said. "Why'd you want to do that?"

Jack Egan's handsome face became a mask of icy fury. "Because it'll kill her, that's why!" he almost shouted. "Because it's the one thing she won't be able to take. It'll tear her apart, shrivel her up like a dried prune. Those goddamn horses are everything to that crazy little bitch, and I'm going to kill every last one of them."

Fargo stared at the man's rage, the throbbing muscles in his jaw, the red scar suddenly grown almost purple. "And if she keeps trying to stop me, I'll save the last bullet for her," Egan added after a pause.

"You're carrying a lot of hate for Prudence Thorpe," Fargo commented.

"That's right," Egan shot back.

"Why take it out on a herd of beautiful and valuable animals?" Fargo asked, trying to keep a line of reason-

71

ableness afloat only to see it founder in the waves of fury that rolled out of Jack Egan.

"You stupid, Fargo? The goddamn horses are the heart of it. It all circles around them. She tried to stop me before, and she's still trying. I get them and I get her, all in one," Egan said, and Fargo watched him raise his hand and touch the scar across his forehead. "You see that, Fargo? She gave me that. Damn near killed me. Marked me for life on our wedding night," he rasped.

Fargo felt the astonishment flood his face. "Your wedding night?" he echoed.

"That's right. I came to collect what was mine. Instead of hot pussy I got a hot poker across the head," the man flung out in bitter anger.

"You telling me Prudence is your wife?" Fargo frowned.

"Not anymore. Never even got her in bed, the wild bitch," Egan said. "After damn near killing me she ran off. She got Judge Howard in Barkerville to give her one of those annulments within a month. Didn't make any damn difference to me. I don't want any part of her. I just aim to pay her back."

Fargo's lips pursed reflectively. "This puts another light on things," he mused aloud. "But it doesn't change the core of it. Those mustang Arabians are too special just to kill off."

"Not to me. Besides, that's none of your concern, 'less you're thinking of helping Prudence Thorpe," Egan said and eyed the big man in front of him.

"Wasn't thinking about it," Fargo said, the answer honest enough.

"Good. Keep it that way," Egan said.

"That a warning?" Fargo asked quietly.

"Friendly advice," Egan said. "Anything else I can do for you?"

"Guess not," Fargo answered. "I'll just be getting along."

"Excuse me for a minute," Jack Egan said. "I just want to check on something." He spun at once, not waiting for a reply, and strode from the room, and Fargo heard the side door open and close. He waited, his thoughts on the conversation with Jack Egan, and he felt his irritation at Prudence. She needed some lessons on telling the whole truth, he grunted. He cut off thoughts as he heard the door open and Egan came into the room. "Sorry for the interruption," the man smiled, his handsome face relaxed again. "Need any supplies, some extra rations?" he asked.

"Nope," Fargo said as he turned to leave. Egan walked outside with him, his smile the spirit of friendliness. The gray-purple of dusk rolled slowly down the distant mountains, Fargo noted.

"You figure to be seeing Prudence Thorpe again?" Egan asked.

"Maybe. It's a small world," Fargo replied noncommittally. He let his eyes go past the man to the stable, move along the fences, the corrals. His face stayed expressionless as he held the small smile inside himself.

"Forget about her and her wild ideas, Fargo," Egan said. "She's crazy."

"I'll try and do that," Fargo answered. He mounted the Ovaro and rode slowly away as Egan watched until he was out of sight. Fargo continued to head south along a small road for another few minutes and then turned the horse in a wide circle and moved north toward the mountains. The dusk had become deep purple when he started up into the mountains, and he paused frequently, seemed to make his way very carefully, and now the tight little smile edged his lips. He rode upward, into the mountain timber, as the dusk turned into the black of night. A half-moon still hung too low in the sky to afford light, and he moved slowly, carefully. At a half-circle beside a stand of ironwood, he halted and made camp, unsaddling the pinto and placing his bedroll alongside the thick-scaled brown bark of the tree trunks. He whistled to himself as he laid out his things, decided against a fire, since the night was warm and a little sticky. He lay down on his bedroll, put his hands behind his head, and closed his eyes.

Slowly, he let the night envelope him, dark and silent at first, and then only dark as the night sounds began to paint their own picture for him. Mule deer, a small group, moved through the trees a dozen yards away. Three raccoons wandered to his left, noisy travelers, and the hoarse, low-pitched, ducklike sound told him a covy of night herons nested nearby. Soft, deliberate steps nearby identified a marten passing. The click and whirring of stag beetles, the soft harvest flies, and the flapping noise of the red bats were all signs that the forest life flowed undisturbed. Fargo continued to lie still, his entire being tuned in on the dark picture that night sounds formed. He had only to wait, he knew, and the answer came finally, a faint, dull stamp, a sound that would have gone unheard by other men. But not by the Trailsman as he remained totally still, listening. The sound came again, a horse's foot restlessly stamping the ground. A horse with shod hoves that added weight and dullness to the sound. More than one horse, he determined. Not very far away. But then they would stay close for the night, he murmured silently.

The grim smile touched his lips again, and he lay still for another few minutes. Finally, he moved, rolling slowly onto his side on the bedroll, then rolling again until he was on the grass. Soft, silent grass. He pushed himself to his feet, using the palms of his hands, began to move on soft cat's steps through the darkness, in the direction the sound of the horse's hoofs had come from.

He'd gone perhaps a dozen yards when he halted, lifted his head, his nostrils widening as he sniffed the air. He drew in deep drafts of the night as he let his nose separate the scents that drifted to him. The faint wintergreen odor of black birch, first, then the sweet-sharp scent of hemlock. The dark, musty odor of damp underbrush drew through his nostrils, and then the odor he sought, the unmistakable smell of saddle leather and horse.

He shifted direction to the right and moved forward again, each step testing, cautious, and soon the figures came into sight, one sitting up against the base of a tree trunk, two others stretched out on the ground. Three, he grunted, and swept the site again with his eyes just to be certain. The half-moon had risen high enough to filter a pale light through the trees as Fargo worked his way toward the figure against the tree trunk. They were all asleep, he saw, as he came up behind the tree and drew the big Colt from his holster. He stepped around the tree, sank into a crouch, and pressed the end of the barrel against the man's temple. The figure came awake at once, sitting up straight. "Don't move," Fargo said softly.

"Jesus," the man said, and Fargo saw the other two figures come awake at once, push themselves to a sitting position. One started to reach for his gun.

"You do that and his head comes off," Fargo warned.

"No . . . Jesus, no," the man cried out. "Nobody's going to do anything. Don't get nervous, mister."

"I'm not the one who's nervous," Fargo said calmly. He reached over and drew the man's gun from its holster as he kept the Colt pressed against his temple. His eyes flicked to the other two men. "Take your guns out, nice and slow, two fingers," he said. The men obeyed after a moment, held the guns up between thumbs and forefingers. Fargo rose, took the Colt from the man's temple.

"Throw the guns over here," he ordered, and the other two men obeyed. He kicked the guns into the brush as the two men rose to their feet. One stood thin and tall as a beanpole; the other was of medium height and sturdy. The third man also got to his feet and stared at the big man with the Colt out of small, sharp eyes.

"How'd you come onto us?" he growled.

Fargo allowed a tight smile. "Hell, I knew you were waiting to follow me before I left Egan's place," he answered.

"How? You didn't see us leave," the man protested.

"Didn't have to," Fargo answered. "Not only was the stable door open when I went outside but it was still swinging. Somebody had ridden out in a big hurry. And two of the saddles on the fence were gone. It didn't take a lot of figuring to put it together. Egan sent you out to wait for me, then follow and learn the way up to the girl's place."

"You're crazy. We just happened to be ridin' up here," the sharp-eyed man said.

"Like hell. What else did Egan tell you to do?" Fargo bit out.

"We don't know what you're talkin' about, mister," the beanpole figure said.

"Bullshit. I want answers. I want to be sure about Jack Egan. What orders did he give you?" Fargo thundered.

"You hard of hearing? Nothing, we told you," the man snarled. The Colt in Fargo's hand barked once, and the beanpole figure leaped into the air in what seem a one-legged rigadoon. "Ow! Jesus, my foot! He shot my god-damn foot!" the man screamed. He seized the smaller man's shoulder for support as he snarled in pain at the big man with the Colt. "You crazy, goddamn you?" he flung out.

"Next time both your kneecaps. What did Egan tell you to do?" Fargo said and raised the Colt.

"No, Jesus, don't!" the man screamed. "I'll tell you."

"Shut up, Slim," the small-eyed man cut in, and Fargo saw the thin one glance at his partner, sudden uncertainty filling his eyes.

Fargo pulled the hammer back on the Colt, the small click sounding immense in the silence of the forest. "You've got two seconds," he said. "One for each kneecap."

The thin man's gaze held on the end of the gun barrel, and the uncertainty in his eyes vanished in a stampede of fear. "He told us to kill you," he said, flinging the words out in a single burst of breath. "But only after we'd followed you all the way to her place."

"You never had any fuckin' guts," the small-eyed man snarled at the thin figure.

"It's not your goddamn kneecaps he's gonna shoot off," the other flung back, still holding his foot in the air. Fargo let his thoughts go to Jack Egan. The thin man's words were not just admission but confirmation, suspicions made certain, evaluations proved out. He had tagged the man correctly. Jack Egan's inhumane, callous disregard for the magnificent horses and their heritage wasn't just rooted in his personal hate for Prudence Thorpe. That was only a fixing point, an added reason, consuming as it was. Jack Egan was a man without regard for anyone or anything but himself, a man who'd order killing as casually as he'd stamp out a cigarette. Fargo had let the thoughts hold him for only a few brief moments, but it was enough for trouble. The small-eyed man, sensing his moment of preoccupation, darted one hand inside his shirt and pulled out a short-barreled .31 caliber pocket pistol, fired off a shot at once. Uttering a silent curse at himself, Fargo had time only to fling himself sideways as he felt the bullet tear through his shirt sleeve. He hit the ground, rolled from a second shot that kicked up the ground inches from his head, and heard the three men diving into the underbrush.

Fargo came up against a tree, swerved himself half behind the trunk, and heard the men in the brush diagonally across from him. "I got the guns," one called out, and Fargo listened to him crawling sideways through the tall brush, the sounds of the others scooting to meet up with him. Fargo stayed motionless and swore at himself again for the single moment of inattention, a mistake that, like most mistakes, would demand payment. He continued to stay in place, listening to their whispered exchanges as they met in the heavy brush. Fargo moved silently back a few paces, flattened himself on the ground beside the base of a staghorn sumac with low-hanging branches, a thick cover of underbrush close against the trunk.

They'd have to come looking for him, he knew, but a prolonged cat-and-mouse game could mean trouble. There was always a chance they'd get lucky. He had to bring them to where he wanted, make them react and be ready to strike. His eyes swept the distant brush, his ears straining to the sounds of movement. The beanpole with the wounded foot would stay in place to cover the half-circle from the front while the other two would try to circle in on him from both sides. He'd help them, he grunted silently. They were no hunters; their reactions were almost predictable. He reached up, his hand circling around a length of new, low branch. He pulled, snapped it off, the sound sharp in the dark forest. He lay flat, the length of thin branch at his side, and listened to the sounds of the two men in the brush. He kicked out with one foot, scraped his heel along the ground, and sent a small stone clattering. He lay quiet again. He'd marked his position for them, and he listened to the sounds as the two men crawled through the brush toward the staghorn sumac, moving too quickly, too anxious to pin him between them.

Fargo slid backward, inching his way in absolute silence, the length of branch in one hand. He paused every few inches to listen. The two gunhands continued to make their way through the brush. His hand touched a stone and he picked it up, tossed it out against the trunk of the sumac. It struck and skittered noisily into the brush to again seem to pinpoint his position. Once more he began the slow inching backward, halting to listen every few moments. His ears again painted a picture for him. Egan's men were performing exactly as he'd intended, zeroing in on him from both sides, the third, bean pole figure staying in place in the distant bushes. Fargo moved back again, keeping himself flat against the ground, and halted finally when he'd moved some six feet from the tree. His face turned on its side against the ground, he waited, listening. The two men pushing through the brush were a clumsy attempt at stealth until they neared the staghorn sumac. They halted then, silence falling with an abruptness, the pale, filtered moon barely outlining the tops of the thick mountain brush.

Fargo lifted his head, brought the Colt forward in his right hand, his left hand curled around the length of tree branch. He rested easily as he let the two men wait, a thin smile brushing his lips. Waiting was a weapon of its own, and he knew the two gunhands were already struggling with impatience. Instead of letting their muscles stay relaxed, as his were, they were tightening, tensing, nerves beginning to push at the edge of self-control. He continued to rest easily in the brush, waiting with the silent patience of a red-tailed hawk, an ability not so much made as mastered.

The two men ran out of patience even sooner than he'd expected, and he heard the one at his left start to move forward again, the other following suit at once. Fargo picked up the movement of the brush as the two men crawled closer to the big sumac. He lifted his arm and tossed the length of branch javelin-fashion. It struck the back of the tree trunk. Instantly, both figures half rose from their cover and poured gunfire into the brush at the base of the tree. Fargo let out a terrible groan, drew the sound from deep in his belly and brought it to an end with a guttural rasp of breath. "We got him," he heard the one shout and saw both figures straighten up, begin to run toward the sumac.

They had acted just as he'd planned for them to act, their moves made of absolute predictability, Fargo snorted inwardly as he aimed the Colt at the figure to his left. He fired, swung the barrel of the revolver sharply to the right, and fired again, the shots a split second apart. Both men shuddered for an instant, but their momentum carried them forward. Both fell headlong at the same instant to land at the base of the tree, their heads touching as the rivers of red ran from their temples to mingle on the grass.

Fargo rose to a half-crouch, listened, and heard the scraping gait of the third man, making his way through the trees, pulling his injured foot along. He had reached the spot where the horses were tethered, Fargo realized, and he stayed in his half-crouch, watched the horses. The man would have to move a horse out at least partly into the open area, and Fargo watched for his shape to appear beside the horses. But he bit down on his lips as he saw the man swing onto one of the horses from the opposite side, flatten himself across the animal's withers, no target in the poor light. Damn, Fargo swore. Once again, he had to make things happen, bank on a predictable reaction. He saw the horse start to bolt forward, and he ran from out of the brush, started to cut in front of the horse as he yelled out a stream of curses. It seemed a move of desperation that presented an open target, and he saw the figure push up from the horse's withers, unable to resist the opportunity that presented itself.

The thin figure fired two shots, too quickly, both wide of their mark, as Fargo dropped to the ground directly in front of the racing horse. The rider had to lean awkwardly out of the saddle to fire, and again his shots were wild. Fargo lay with palms pressed hard onto the ground, holding his position for another half second as the horse bore down on him. As the animal's thundering forefeet were raised to come down on him, he pushed hard, using every steel-spring muscle in his arms and shoulders to fling himself to one side. He felt the rush of air on his face as the horse thundered past him, and he rolled, came up with the Colt in one hand as he lay on the ground. As he had expected, the rider pulled back on the reins, half turned in the saddle to see if horse or bullets had struck their mark. Fargo's Colt barked once, a final exclamation point for predictability. The tall, thin figure seemed to stretch taller as the man's back arched and he toppled from saddle, hitting the horse's rump as he fell to the ground. He lay still, not unlike a broken bulrush beside a pond.

Fargo rose to his feet, drew a deep breath as he holstered the Colt. In grim silence, he moved through the woods, gathering in the horses and dragging the three lifeless forms to the center of the tiny clear place. He lifted each, draped each silent form over a horse, and tied them on with their lariats. He swung onto his horse and gathered the reins of the other three horses together and began to move down from the mountain timber. He rode slowly, back to the low plains and Jack Egan's ranch. The night was deep, the moon already on its curving path toward the horizon when he rode into the Egan place. He led the grisly procession to the front of the ranchhouse and tied the horses side by side at the hitching post. He turned the pinto and rode away as silently as he had arrived. Only when the ranch was out of sight did he turn the pinto into a trot.

Jack Egan would find the grim message come morning, and he'd know it was more than simply a defiant gesture. He'd know its meaning, understand it was not just an answer but a statement. The chips had been tossed, and there'd be no cashing in now, not until the game was over. Jack Egan would see to that.

Fargo rode back the way he had come, into the mountain country, found a big alder with a wide spread of branches and bedded down. He slept heavily and didn't wake till the sun was high and hot. He washed in the cool of a mountain stream and remembered his way up into the Beartooth Mountains, paying close attention to the markings he'd carefully noted in his mind. The sun had swung into midafternoon when he reached the cabin. No one emerged to greet him, and the door hung open. The chestnut was gone, he noted, as he corralled the pinto. He went into the cabin, found some beef jerky, and filled the emptiness that had gathered in his stomach. The mountains were taking on the deep lilac of dusk when Prudence rode up to the cabin. She'd see the Ovaro at once, he knew, and he stepped outside as she dismounted, unsaddled the chestnut, and put the horse into the small corral. She finally turned to him, the sage-green eyes holding a kind of belligerent curiosity.

"Why did you come back? I told you I wouldn't care what Jack Egan said," she tossed out.

"It's not so much what he said as what you didn't say," Fargo remarked.

The green eyes narrowed. "Such as?" she answered.

"There's more than just the mustangs here. There's a well full of hating," Fargo said.

"That doesn't change what he is. It just makes it

worse," she said, the answer true enough, Fargo admitted silently.

"How'd it come to that?" Fargo questioned.

"My marrying him?" Prudence asked, and he nodded. She thought back for a moment, her lips pressing tight onto each other. "His being a handsome bastard, my being a naive fool," she bit out.

"Fill it in some," Fargo said.

"He is handsome, you saw that," Prudence began. "And he can be smooth and dashing. He romanced me with a rush. I'll admit I wasn't the most experienced girl around. Men usually didn't measure up to what I wanted. Either they were good-looking and insensitive or sensitive and unattractive. But mostly, they didn't understand me, how I feel about the wild things."

"And Jack Egan did?" Fargo said.

"He made me believe he did. He knew I knew about the mustangs and I was about the only person who knew where they roamed. He convinced me he wanted the same thing for them that I did," Prudence said and paused in thought for a moment. "Thank God I held back telling him everything. Something must have warned me inside," she went on. "Though I did believe him. I guess I wanted to believe him so very much."

"What happened?" Fargo pressed.

"The afternoon we were married I overheard him talking to his foreman, a man named Coley," Prudence said.

"The late Mr. Coley," Fargo cut in, and her brows arched for a moment.

"I learned the truth. He was going to use me and the Arabians whatever way he wanted. I heard him tell Coley how the marriage was a business investment for him. What he really wanted was to get his hands on those Arabians," Prudence said. "The rotten bastard came to me that night. Imagine, he thought he could have me after what I'd learned. He found out different."

"Yes, he pointed that out to me," Fargo said.

"So that was it," Prudence said, her eyes studying him. "What difference would it have made if I'd told you?" she asked.

"I might have tried a different approach. I sure wouldn't have tried talking sweet reasonableness to a man filled with that kind of hate. I'd have known better than to stick my neck out like that. The point is, you lied to me, and I don't like being lied to," Fargo said.

"I didn't lie," she snapped.

"You didn't tell all of it. That's another kind of lying, and I ought to fan your little ass for it," he growled.

She glared at him, no concession in her stare. "You come all the way back just to say that?" she muttered.

"No," he said.

"What, then?" she frowned belligerently.

"Guess I decided those mustang Arabians deserve to stay free, and you sure as hell won't keep them that way alone," Fargo said.

She studied him, waited, turned thoughts inside her. The wariness clung as she finally answered. "I'll pay, if you're not wanting too much," she said.

"You doing this for money?" he asked.

"Of course not," she bristled at once. "You know that."

"The money's not part of it for me, either, not for this," he said.

"I'm not offering anything else," she snapped.

He laughed quietly. "Didn't figure you would. That wouldn't make me come back."

"Hell, you say. I've seen your eyes take me in, Mr. Fargo," she flared.

"They have. You're a good-looking girl, Miss Thorpe," he conceded. "But I've no time for teaching or taming," he added with a laugh.

The anger blazed in her eyes at once. "Go to hell,

Fargo. I don't need the first and you couldn't do the second," she flung back.

"That shows one thing, at least," he said mildly.

"What?" she frowned.

"You can be wrong twice in the same breath," he grinned. Her lips tightened, and she brushed past him as she strode into the cabin. He followed, watched her put a fat-bellied coffeepot on the fire. She dug into a wooden box and pulled out a parcel wrapped in burlap that turned out to be cooked and preserved hare.

"This'll be enough for dinner tonight. You can use that fancy shooting eye of yours to get us something for tomorrow," she said.

He nodded and took the big Sharps rifle with him as he went outside. He walked along the top of a low ridge in the rapidly gathering dusk and was grateful to bring down two ruffed grouse before the light failed. It was after they'd eaten and the night cloaked the cabin that he asked the questions he'd gathered inside himself as Prudence plucked the grouse, singeing off feathers in the fire.

"The Kiowa ride this territory. So do the Arapaho and the Crow. How come they've left you alone?" he questioned.

"I don't know. They've watched me. I've seen them doing it," Prudence answered. "Maybe, in some way, they understand what I'm doing."

Fargo turned her words in his mind. He wouldn't laugh them away. He'd seen stranger things. Yet experience told him that the Indians were simply watching and waiting, perhaps wondering. He went on to other items in his mind. "You talked about plans. What kind of plans?" he asked.

"The best I could manage. I'll show you tomorrow," she said.

"No more surprises," he warned. "If I'm going to stay I want to know whatever there is to know."

She nodded, rose, and put the grouse into a wooden storage box. The fire had begun to burn itself out. The night remained warm enough to do without the fire, and Prudence cleaned up the plucked feathers. "One of us sleeps outside one night, the other the next night. We'll take turns," she said primly.

"You keep the bed. I'll use the floor," Fargo said.

"No," she said quickly. "We'll draw straws for who gets the bed tonight."

"It's raining outside. I'm taking the floor," Fargo said.

She spun, pulled the door open, and frowned at the rain that tried to blow into the cabin at once. She pushed the door shut, stared at Fargo with astonishment lacing the frown. "Remarkable," she murmured.

"Educated ears," he said as he rose and took his sleeping blanket and began to spread it on the floor in front of the dying fire. He glanced at her as she watched, standing stiffly, uncertainty in her eyes. "You afraid to sleep in the same room with a man?" he asked with a slow smile.

"I'm not afraid," she said, drawing herself together. "I'm not afraid of anything."

"Except yourself," he laughed as he began to take his shirt off.

"You've no cause to say that," she flared. "You don't know anything about me."

"I know enough," he smiled and pulled the shirt off. She turned away as he began to unbutton his trousers but not before he'd watched her eyes move across the hard-muscled beauty of his chest. She turned her back to him as he undressed, stayed that way until she heard him roll the blanket around himself.

"I suppose it's useless to ask you not to watch if I undress here," she said.

"Yep," he smiled happily.

She sniffed indignantly and turned away, swung onto the bed, and lifted the sheet high enough to form a small tent. He watched her stay behind her makeshift tent until she dropped the sheet to emerge cloaked in a long, blue-gray flannel nightgown. Her glance was made of smug satisfaction in the last of the flickering firelight. "Goodnight," she said with annoyance still in her voice.

" 'Night," he answered. He closed his eyes and turned on his side. The last of the fire sputtered away and the cabin became black. He'd almost fallen asleep when he heard her voice, quiet, the thorns gone from it.

"Fargo . . . thanks for coming back," she said.

He grunted acceptance and let sleep close out the world as outside the rain continued to fall in a steady, earth-soaking downpour.

6

She seemed to take in the wind as though she were part of it, high-planed face raised up, eyes half closed. He watched her from inside the cabin as she stood on a small mound of earth, blouse and skirt blown tight against her to give contours to long, slender legs and the rise of her modest breasts. The rain had stopped come the morning, but the day was gray and windy, the earth soaked soft, and she'd left the cabin to stand outside. She turned abruptly, suddenly aware of his eyes on her.

"Let's go," she called back as she strode to the chestnut in the corral and began to saddle the horse. Fargo readied the Ovaro, followed after her as she started a brisk trot, winding the circuitous path up toward the mountain plateau. He was a half-dozen feet behind her when he saw her veer and head toward a steep incline dotted with saplings and rock. The steep grade led to a high ridge.

"Shortcut," she called back.

"Don't try it," he said.

She paused only to toss a slightly pained glance back

at him. "My horse can do it, and if he can so can yours," she said, and pushed the chestnut up the incline with a surge. Fargo veered and followed, and the oath stayed inside himself as he reached the bottom of the incline. He let the pinto move up a dozen steps, his mouth tightening. He pulled the pinto to a halt, looked ahead to see Prudence clinging to the chestnut as the horse had trouble with his footing. She'd gone only a dozen yards when the ground gave way, a quick sucking noise, sliding down from under the horse, earth, rock, and young saplings going with it. The small slide loosened the ground above it, the incline sliding down over itself. Fargo saw the chestnut fall, slide with the earth, Prudence thrown clear. A sapling came against her, turned her half over as she tumbled downward with earth, branches, and rock. Fargo spurred the Ovaro sideways, the horse on level enough ground to keep a firm footing. Prudence's form, arms tossed outward, came toward him, a piece of rock gaining on her. He reached down as she came past him, got one hand around her arm, and yanked hard. She came up with a small shower of earth, and he leaned over, got his other arm around her waist, lifted her high against him as the pinto moved away from the slide. The horse halted a yard or two from the small slide on firm ground, and Prudence stayed with her arms around the big man's neck.

He held her, felt the softness of her and drew in the warm smell of her as she clung to him. Her breath came in quick drafts, and she slowly began to breathe easier. He felt her push against him, a small movement he ignored. "I'm all right now," she murmured into his chest.

"You sure?" he asked and he caught the extra pause before she answered.

"Yes, quite sure," she said. He held on to her. "I'm all right," she said.

"So am I," he said blandly. Her hands pushed harder against him, and he loosened his grip and let her slide down to the ground, his eyes made of quiet laughter.

"Thanks," she said gravely. "That's getting to be a habit, isn't it?"

"Maybe you ought to listen once in a while," he told her without gentleness. "Or think more," he added. He saw her mouth tighten as she turned to find the chestnut where he had regained his feet and was shaking dirt and twigs from his coat.

"I'll try," she snapped as she strode to the horse. He swung in just behind her as she started to ride up the winding paths until the mountain plateau came into sight. The mustangs were there, ears up in alertness at once as the two riders halted at the edge of the plain. The horses were moving restlessly under the low-scudding gray clouds, and Prudence halted, her eyes moving back and forth across the pack. Fargo watched her toss her head in the wind, the gesture almost an echo of a buff-colored mare that tossed her mane. Suddenly he wasn't there, Fargo realized. She was alone with the wild horses, a silent exchanging. Finally, she returned to his presence, her eyes shining.

"I don't see the Wild Shadow," Fargo said.

"He's near," she answered. "I can feel it." She'd hardly finished the words when he saw the ebony stallion appear on a distant ledge to stand majestically, his sensitive, fine-lined profile sniffing the air. The sun broke through the clouds with almost startling suddenness to flood the plateau with new warmth, and the wind vanished with the last of the racing clouds. Fargo watched the wild stallion leap from the ledge and move through the herd with stately majesty. "They come here all the time, too many of them," Prudence said.

"Too many?" Fargo echoed.

"If Egan comes chasing after them they'll come here,"

she said and gestured to the narrow end of the plateau where a face of steep rock rose almost perpendicularly into the air. "He'll no doubt seal off the other end of the plateau with his men. With that rock at this end and his riders sealing off the other end he'll have the herd boxed in," she said.

"Just about," Fargo said. Prudence beckoned to him and moved her horse around the edge of the mountain plateau until she reached the end where the rock rose steep and clifflike. She halted, and he followed her gaze to see a narrow passageway that cut through the otherwise solid face of sheer stone.

"That go all the way through?" Fargo asked.

"It will when I'm finished," Prudence said.

He frowned. "You didn't dig this, sweetie, not unless you had an army of helpers," he said.

"No, I didn't dig it, but I've about cleared it," Prudence said. "It's a passage that's been filled with rock fallen into it from up on top, years and years of it." She moved forward into the narrow defile, and he followed, the space just large enough for one, perhaps two horses to fit through side by side. He took in the rocks placed neatly along both sides of the passageway and halted the pinto as a small wall of rock loomed up. "Been at it for a month," Prudence said. "Every day. Stinking, back-breaking work." He saw the shovel and pick standing against the wall of rock still to be cleared. "Ready to work?" she said as she started to clamber up on the mound of stone. "We can finish in a few days with the two of us at it," she said.

"Where does it come out?" he asked as he dismounted.

"Onto land that's half open and half timber," she said. "The main thing is it'll give them a way out. He won't be able to box them in. They'll be able to get out and scatter."

"That's once. What happens after? Egan's not going to

91

back off once he's found his way up here," Fargo said as he started to pull rocks down alongside her.

Her face grew serious. "I don't know. I'll have to meet that when it happens," she said.

"No good," Fargo said. "There won't be time for improvising. You've got to be ready with a countermove, something that'll be hard and fast." He rolled a large rock down from the mound and paused, the sun burning down into the narrow, stone-lined passage. "We finish opening this passage and then I'll want to ride the land till I know every inch of it. I'll have to figure a way to hit back." He paused to gaze down the remainder of the narrow defile. "You're counting on that black stallion to lead them through this passage," he said.

"He will. The Wild Shadow is their leader. They'll follow wherever he takes them," Prudence said.

Fargo straightened up and felt the sun beating down hard. He pulled his shirt off and returned to work, carrying and rolling the loose rocks down to line the edges of the passage. His body glistened with perspiration, every muscle coated to stand out in magnificent symmetry. He caught Prudence pausing to watch him, twice, and each time she quickly looked away. By afternoon her blouse, soaked with perspiration, clung to her to outline the softly rounded contours of each breast. Fargo ran a hand across his bare-muscled chest. "Join me," he said. "You might as well the way that shirt's sticking to you."

"Sticking's better than showing," she said tartly. He grinned and returned to the backbreaking work. She called a halt when dusk began to gather, and he felt the soreness in his back and shoulders, muscles strained beyond their normal use. He saw Prudence moving carefully, too, as they returned to the cabin. He let her wash and change shirts at the well, first, then took his turn as she tended the grouse over the fire. They ate soon after, and when they finished he watched Prudence take a small

92

cork-topped jar from among her things. "Liniment," she said. "Wonderful for aching muscles. Olive oil, camomile lotion, and apricot kernel. You can use it when I'm finished."

She started for the door, and he called to her, "Now, how in hell are you going to rub your back and shoulders by yourself?" he asked.

"I'm used to it. It's not real good doing it alone, but I do as best I can," she answered. He bounded forward, blocked her way to the door.

"Lay down on the bed, dammit. I'll do you," he said.

She hesitated, her lips pressing against each other. "No," she said. "You've sly ways, but I'm on to that kind of trick."

He reached out, took hold of her shoulder, and spun her around, pushed her down on the bed. "Dammit, you're on to nothing but your own imagination. Now turn over and undo that damn shirt. I'll do you and then you can do me. Fair enough?" he said.

She frowned up at him. "Nothing more," she muttered.

"Nothing more. Christ, I've turned down better shapes than yours," he said as she flipped onto her stomach.

"Mine will do me just fine," she said. He lifted her shirt up to bunch it around her neck and enjoyed a lovely, shapely back, nice shoulder blades that topped a slender contour. He rubbed the tight knots in the muscles at the base of her neck, massaged the shoulder muscles, molded and kneaded and rubbed. The liniment bore a sweet odor and worked its way smoothly into the skin. When he finished and sat back, she pulled the shirt down, had it buttoned properly before she turned around. She took the liniment jar from him and he stripped his shirt off, stretched out on the firm bed. She had a good touch, strong without being rough, and he felt the ointment cool his burning muscles. He turned over for her to rub the material into his pectoral muscles and watched her face as she rubbed her hands over his chest, down along his rib cage, and then back to his shoulders. She refused to lift her eyes to his, kept her gaze concentrated on his chest as she massaged the ointment over him, but he saw her lips had opened in a faint hiss of breath. When she finished, her eyes still not meeting his, he brought his hand up to rest against the small of her back. He pressed, started to bend her forward toward him. She moved with the pressure of his hand and then stiffened, her face growing tight.

"No," she said. "Nothing more, I told you that."

He took his hand from her back. "So you did. What did you tell yourself?" he laughed.

"I didn't have to tell myself anything," she protested.

"The hell you didn't," he laughed again as he sat up. He swung from the bed as he brushed her cheek with his hand, a gesture both casual and intimate. "Sleep tight," he said and began to pull off trousers. She turned away quickly, formed the little tent with the bedsheet, and undressed beneath it, emerging in the blue-gray nightgown. Fargo stretched out on the blanket and felt the ointment working, soothing strained muscles. The last of the fire flickered out to plunge the little cabin into darkness. He lay still, and suddenly her voice cut through the silent dark, indignant anger in each word.

"You've a damn nerve, Fargo. What makes you think you know me?" she flung out.

"They call me the Trailsman," he said.

"What's that mean?" she returned.

"People and trails, they're not all that different. You read the signs on each. You have to understand what they mean," he said.

Icy sarcasm came into her voice. "And you never read them wrong, of course," she said.

"Not often and not this time," he answered and knew she'd hear the amusement in his voice.

"Goodnight," she said with more asperity than concern. He heard her flounce herself, and he closed his eyes and slept in minutes.

Her mood seemed to darken in sleep, for she made the morning a silent time, nodding to him as he emerged from the cabin. She remained silent, her face carrying a glower, as they made their way up to the mountain plateau. "Cat got your tongue this morning?" he asked.

"No," she said firmly, the one-word reply her only comment.

"Fine with me," he shrugged. "I hate prattling females." She gave no answer, and they reached the plateau, where the Arabians turned almost as one. Fargo saw the wild black stallion move through the others to halt in front of the herd, paw the ground with one foot. It was only then that Prudence half turned in the saddle, the words bursting from her.

"You think I'm some kind of prude, don't you?" she accused.

"Your word, not mine," Fargo said and met the anger in her eyes.

"You think it, though," she insisted. "Well, let me tell you something. Being a prude is one thing. Having principles is another."

Not giving him time to answer, she sent the chestnut forward onto the plateau, racing directly at the mustangs. Fargo watched the ebony stallion detach himself from the others and come forward to meet the girl. Prudence halted, slid from the horse, and walked a half-dozen yards to where the big stallion had come to a standstill. Fargo watched as she laid both hands against the horse, moved to lean against the point of his shoulder. She stayed motionless for a moment, then pulled herself onto the ebony back, and the stallion turned at once to become a black streak racing through the herd. Prudence rode with her hand dug into the long mane, her head back, her face lifted to the sun, excitement coursing through her and the wild beauty of her matching the wild stallion's magnificence. It was the horse that decided when the moment was to end, and he came to a halt almost at the spot where she'd climbed onto his back. Prudence slid to the ground, and the stallion backed from her, turned, and trotted to the rest of the herd. Prudence climbed onto the chestnut and rode back to where Fargo waited, wheeled the horse past him, and in her face he saw defiance, anger, wild excitement. She headed for the passageway at the far end of the plateau, and he followed her into the defile, reined up where they had halted work the day before.

Prudence, out of the saddle, had already begun to pull at the rocks, plunging into the task as though the mound of rock were an enemy. Fargo bent to work beside her, watched her as she continued her furious pace. He saw her fighting off the enervating effects of the hot sun, driving herself until, almost at the morning's end, he saw her sway, drop a rock she'd been trying to lift. She almost fell as he caught her, and she came against him, her blouse wet with perspiration, her forehead shiny and hot against his chest. She leaned against him, drew in deep breaths. "I wondered how long before this'd happen," he remarked. She made no reply, stayed inside the strength of his arms until finally she pushed back to peer at him.

"Nothing to say?" she muttered.

"Would you listen?" he asked.

"Probably not," she conceded. "I'm not like most women."

"That's sure as hell the truth," Fargo grunted.

"What I mean is I'm not the kind who'll go jumping into bed with you, no matter how grateful I am for your help," she said.

"I know that," Fargo said affably.

"You do? Good," she said with some surprise.

"Wanting, not gratefulness, will be the reason," he said cheerfully and saw the exasperation flood her face. She stepped back and spun on her heel.

"Let's get back to work," she snapped, and Fargo nodded cheerfully. She resumed pulling down rock, this time at a more normal pace, and the day was nearing a close when suddenly the narrow passageway opened up clear, the land at the other end coming into view. Fargo admitted to a feeling of satisfaction as he swung onto the Ovaro and rode from the narrow defile with Prudence. "Now they won't be trapped," she said.

Fargo scanned the land at the other end of the passage, open areas and plenty of timber, as Prudence had described it. More high ridges and long slopes than she'd said, he noted, and his eyes narrowed in thought as he gazed up to the top of the sheer rock that rose above the end of the passageway as it did at the beginning by the plateau. "What are you thinking?" he heard Prudence ask.

"Tell you when I've thought some more," he answered. He looked at Prudence and saw her stretch her body backward in the saddle. The gesture brought the ache of his own back and shoulder muscles to the fore. The night had already started down the mountains like a black curtain, and he turned the Ovaro to the passageway. "Let's move," he said, and Prudence followed him as he rode back through the cleared passage, which had already grown inky black. They emerged on the high plateau, the mustangs moving shapes in the dark, skirted the flatland, and made their way back to the cabin. He made a small fire, just large enough to roast the other grouse, and when they'd finished eating he lay back on the blanket, watched Prudence as she eased herself down on the edge of the bed.

"Want me to rub your back again?" he asked.

"No," she said, but he'd caught the faint moment of hesitation. "I'm not sore tonight."

"Strange," he mused aloud. "I'm sure feeling it. I'm tired enough to sleep right now." He half rose, started to undress in the flickering firelight. She looked away, he saw, only when he began to pull off his trousers. He stretched out on the blanket in shorts, turned on his side, his back to her. The few low flames still lapping at the logs had almost put him to sleep when he heard her soft steps, lifted his head, half turned to see her sink down on her knees beside him, the jar of ointment in her hand. She pressed him onto his stomach and began to massage his back with the lotion, soothing, strong hands moving gently. He turned on his back after a spell and watched her as she concentrated on her massaging, avoiding his eyes, her hands pressing into his powerful pectoral muscles, moving down along the side of his chest, rubbing with an almost caressing motion. But this time when she finished and corked the jar, he sat up, took her shoulders in his hands.

"No," she breathed instantly. "I told you no." He pulled her to him, pressed his mouth over hers, cutting off further words. He pressed her lips open, felt her mouth soften, tighten, soften again. He pushed her down, came half over her. She murmured, protested, and he felt her hands become fists, dig into his chest as she pushed against him. But her lips stayed half opened, soft, even as she tried to twist away from his mouth. He pulled back with suddenness and saw the surprise touch her eyes as she sat up, let anger push away the surprise.

"Just saying thank you," he smiled cheerfully.

"Use words next time," she flung back hotly.

"I like my way better," he said.

"I don't," she muttered.

"Be careful," he smiled, and she frowned in question.

98

"You'll have me believing you," he chuckled as he stretched out on the blanket. She uttered a snort of impatience, pushed herself to her feet to stride to the bed. The fire snuffed itself out, and Fargo heard her undress in the dark of the room and climb into the bed. He closed his eyes and slept, and the world slowly circled its way to morning.

He woke first when day came, put coffee on, and washed with the well water outside. He'd just finished when Prudence appeared, brushing hair from her face, carrying a towel over one arm. Her chin rose at once as she saw him still in shorts. Her glance flicked over his body, became disapproving as she brushed past him. "I'll pour the coffee," he said.

"After you put some clothes on," she sniffed. He smiled inwardly as he went into the cabin and dressed, had two mugs of the coffee poured when she returned, face still damp with the cold well water, and she brushed her hair with one hand as she sat down. The pure, wild beauty of her sparkled, no powders or rouges to intrude.

"Any more chores?" he asked.

"Only for me," she said. "I started a head count of all the Arabians in this part of the mountains. I stopped to work on the passageway, but now I want to finish."

"You want me to help?" he asked.

She thought for a moment. "No, I think I'd do better alone. I don't want them getting frightened," she said.

Fargo sipped his coffee. "All right, you count, and I'll have a look at the country, someplace to stand against Egan." He'd taken another sip of coffee when he heard the sound, a horse blowing air. He was on one knee in the doorway in seconds, the Colt in his hand. He felt the frown come over his face as he saw the horse move out of the trees toward the cabin, limping badly on its left hind leg. A girl sat the saddle, a girl with dark-brown hair, a brown cape wrapped around her shoulders.

"It's Dolly," he heard Prudence say, and he turned a questioning glance at her. "I told you I get information about Jack Egan. Dolly brings it to me," Prudence said and brushed past him to hurry from the cabin. He rose, holstered the Colt, and followed her outside as the girl eased herself from the horse. Dolly had a round face, too much makeup around brown eyes, full lips, and a nose a little too large. She was attractive enough in an open, eager way, and she took the cape off as she reached the ground to reveal a white scoop-neck blouse which barely contained large, very round breasts that spilled up over the neckline. He saw Dolly's eyes go past Prudence to rest on him.

"Well, you've been holding out on me, Prudence," Dolly said with undisguised appreciation in her eyes.

"This is Fargo," Prudence said.

"Fargo?" Dolly echoed as her eyes continued to gaze at the big black-haired man with open approval. She spoke to Prudence while keeping her eyes on Fargo. "Did I interrupt something?" she asked pointedly.

"No, you definitely did not interrupt anything," Prudence snapped stiffly.

"I don't know why," Dolly said, turning her eyes to Prudence. "This is quite a hunk of man, honey."

"Fargo's here to help me fight Egan," Prudence said.

"Swell, but I could find more use for him than just that," Dolly said.

"Well, I can't," Prudence said stiffly. "My mind isn't on a single track."

"How come you're feeding information to Prudence?" Fargo asked the girl.

"Jack Egan did my brother real dirty, and I'm paying him back," she said. "I work at the dancehall in Threadneedle."

"Dolly hears a lot there, maybe just about everything

100

there is to hear. Threadneedle's not a big town," Prudence put in.

Fargo saw Dolly smile and her eyes twinkle at him. "Fargo's familiar with Threadneedle," she said, and her little laugh was low and sensuous. Her large breasts jiggled as she laughed, lifting to fold over the top of the neckline of the blouse. "Fargo's the one who took apart Humphrey Wills's little racket," Dolly said. "Right, big man?" Fargo nodded. "There's been talk about it ever since. Did a job on that little bitch daughter of his, too, I hear." She laughed again.

"Penny was at the heart of it," Fargo said.

"She can't be the virgin princess anymore, and she's not that good an actress to fake it," Dolly said.

"My, you two have a lot of reminiscences for having just met," Prudence cut in, her voice taking on a waspish edge. "What do you have for me, Dolly?" she added more severely.

Dolly took her eyes from Fargo for a moment. "Nothing good. Egan's hired himself a small army," she said and returned her gaze to the big man in front of her. "Does Jack Egan know you're up here helping Prudence?" she asked.

"He knows," Fargo said.

"That explains it," Dolly said. "He must've told Humphrey Wills, because Wills has joined him with some of his men."

"Figures," Fargo said, his smile tight. "Got any ideas how many men Egan's got together?"

"Fifteen, maybe twenty, a small army, I told you," Dolly said.

Fargo made a face. "Too many. We've got to figure a way to hit back," he said.

"He's not here yet. It'll take him days to find his way, maybe weeks. I want to finish my head count. That way

I'll know if he's taken any along the way," Prudence said.

"Don't be too sure," Dolly answered. "He's got a scouting force moving on first to find the way. They almost found me last night, five of them."

"You going to rest the morning before starting back as usual?" Prudence asked Dolly.

"Yes, only I might not go back. I don't want to run into Egan's scouting force, and my horse went lame all of a sudden," Dolly said.

"I think you should go back. I'm sure you won't run into Egan's men," Prudence said. "You'll be safer back in town than up here."

Dolly shot Fargo a wide smile. "It might be more fun up here," she said.

"No," Prudence snapped sharply. "I can't be watching out for your neck. Get some rest and go back."

"I'll take a look at your horse," Fargo said, and Dolly shrugged as he went to the dark-brown gelding and lifted the animal's left hind hoof for a closer look. He put it down gently after a moment and rubbed his hand along the horse's leg from the cannon bone down to the fetlock and along the pastern. "The shoe's half off," he said, straightening up. "That's what started his limping, but the limping has swollen the leg and pastern. I can fix the shoe on tight enough to hold till you can get to a smithy, but that swelling has to come down before you can ride back."

"How long will that take?" Prudence asked.

"With cold compresses, I'd guess about four hours, at least," Fargo answered.

"Looks as though I'll be staying awhile," Dolly said, and her glance went back and forth between Prudence and the big man. "You sure I'm not interrupting anything?" she questioned.

"I told you, most definitely not," Prudence snapped.

Dolly's face mirrored incomprehension. "Whatever you say, Prudence," she returned and tossed Fargo a wide smile. "I'll get a few hours' sleep inside. This all-night riding does me in," she yawned.

Prudence went to the corral and brought the chestnut out. "You coming with me?" she said to Fargo.

He let the mild surprise show in his face. "I offered before and you said it'd be best if you went alone," he reminded her.

Prudence blinked, turned to finish saddling the horse. "So I did," she said, her voice tight.

"I'll take the time to work on the shoe and the swelling on the gelding's leg," Fargo said.

"Do that," Prudence snapped, swung onto the chestnut, and sent the horse off in a fast trot.

Dolly stared after her till she disappeared over a rise and returned her gaze to Fargo, her eyes narrowed, questioning. "You sure I didn't interrupt anything?" she asked once again.

"You heard the lady," Fargo said.

"Yes, I heard her," Dolly echoed. "Strange one, that Prudence Thorpe. Not somebody I've anything much in common with."

"I imagine not," Fargo agreed.

"Except hating Jack Egan, and that's enough for us both," Dolly said. She started for the cabin, and Fargo watched the way her breasts swayed under the blouse. Dolly's little smile was edged with something unsaid, and her eyes twinkled. "Don't go 'way. I won't be sleeping long," she said.

"Wouldn't think of it," he grinned back. He watched as she walked into the cabin, nice, full rear, a rounded figure, perhaps ten pounds too much on her but she was young enough to carry it off.

He turned and scouted the area until he found a stone flat enough and heavy enough to suit his purpose. Using

103

it as a hammer, he began work on the horse's shoe. He managed to hammer the remaining nails into the shoe so they'd hold it on the hoof for a few hours of normal riding. It was slow work, his makeshift hammer unwieldy to use. When he finally finished the shoe he went to the well with a towel, soaked it in water, and bandaged the swollen area of the leg. He lay down near the horse and thought about Jack Egan between half-hour trips to the well to put on fresh, cool bandages. One fact emerged from his musings. There'd be no holding off fifteen or twenty gunslingers without finding a way to neutralize their firepower. A vague plan nibbled at his thoughts. He'd need to examine the high land on both sides of the narrow mountain defile they had cleared, he pondered as he rose to refresh the towel around the horse's leg.

The swelling had gone down appreciably, he noted with satisfaction, and he had just rewrapped the pastern area when Dolly emerged from the cabin, one hand rubbing sleep from her eyes. She waved at him as she walked to the well, pumped the bucket full of water. As he watched, she pulled the white blouse over her head and her breasts cascaded free, tremendously full and pillowy, perhaps too much of a good thing, Fargo commented silently. Another few years and they'd be sagging cowlike, he reflected. She pushed her skirt off to stand naked beside the well, a round, full rear, full-fleshed thighs, a young peasant girl's figure, perhaps a little coarse yet throbbing with vitality. She lifted the bucket, poured the water over herself, and Fargo watched the little droplets glisten along her back and buttocks in the hot sun.

Dolly turned to him, waiting, a little bulge to her belly above a dense triangle. He walked toward her, and she lifted her arms when he reached her, closed them around his neck. His hands circled her back, her skin still wet, very smooth. Her mouth came on his, open, a sucking kiss, and he felt the cushiony softness of her big breasts against his chest. She stepped back, moved toward the trees beside the cabin, and he followed, unbuttoning his shirt. She halted in a sun-flecked little glade with a bed of thick, green Indian ricegrass, lay down at once as he shed the last of his clothes to kneel down beside her. He watched her eyes stay on his maleness, powerfully erect, quick to respond to the sight of her full-fleshed sensuous waiting. "Oh, Jesus," Dolly breathed, and fell back, her fleshy thighs opening at once.

Her hand reached out, took hold of him, stroking, pulling him to her. "Oh, Jesus," she said again as she held him, guided him to her. She was quickly wet, flowing, welcoming, and pushed upward as he entered her. His face came down onto the cushiony breasts, terribly soft, almost touching flabbiness yet clinging to youthful strength, encompassing, enveloping, sweet refuge. He slid forward in her, and Dolly cried out. "Yes, oh, Jesus, yes . . . aaaaah . . ." she breathed, pure sexual pleasure filling her voice. Her hands clasped around his back, and he felt her legs lift to circle behind his legs, push forward in rhythm as he began to pump inside her. He heard her laugh, the low, sexy sound, a laugh of unalloyed enjoyment. No subtleties for Dolly, no soft caresses or sweet murmurings. Yet her pure, open enjoyment brought its own kind of pleasure, a one-layered but totally consuming joy in sex.

She thrust back with him, laughed in pleasure, gasped out happy little sounds. "Ah . . . ah, Christ, oh, that's good . . . that's good, yes . . . oh, Jesus," she breathed, urgings, approvals, exhortations, and her hands pushed his face into and over and against the pillowed breasts. He felt the fleshy little belly suddenly push hard against him and her thighs tightened. He thrust quickly, roughly, caught up to her hurried coming, and exploded with her. "Oh, holy God . . . aaaiiiiiii," she screamed and pressed him tight against her until, slowly, she sank back-

105

ward onto the grass and he watched her big breasts heave up and down as she regained breath.

"Damn, that was somethin' special," Dolly breathed against him as he lay half over her. "I knew it would be the minute I laid eyes on you."

"You can't tell a book by its cover," he said.

"Maybe I can't tell books, but I can tell men," Dolly laughed. She pulled his face down onto one soft breast, and he'd just opened his lips around the large nipple when he heard the sound, brush being moved, and he pulled away, rolled from her, one hand reaching out to find the Colt on the ground nearby, when he saw the figure come through the trees, the rifle in hand.

"Dammit. I knew it, I just knew it," he heard Prudence say, and he sat up as she stepped into the little glade. He saw her fury in the tight set of her face, the sage-green eyes blazing yet pausing to take in his naked maleness still half erect. She tore her glance away to focus on Dolly's soft white flesh. "Goddammit, get your clothes on, both of you," Prudence barked, and Fargo saw she held the rifle so tightly her knuckles were white. "Get up and get dressed, dammit," Prudence said again, and her voice rose in fury.

"What the hell are you so mad about?" Dolly said as she sat up, pulled her blouse toward her.

"Just get dressed and get out of here," Prudence said. She turned to Fargo. "You too, damn you," she snapped. "You're like all the others, ready to jump into the hay with anyone, anytime, anyplace."

Dolly's voice cut in before he could say anything. "Damn if you're not jealous. You should've told me you were saving him for yourself," she said.

Prudence blazed fury at her. "I wasn't saving him for myself and I'm not jealous," she shouted.

Dolly started from the glade. "Shit you're not," she threw back over her shoulder. Prudence shot a furious glare at Fargo as he drew on trousers, and his half-shrug added new anger to the sage-green eyes.

"You'd agree, of course," Prudence said. "Well, you can get out too. Go with her. Enjoy yourselves."

"I'm staying," he said quietly as he strapped on his gunbelt.

"Don't bother. I don't need you," Prudence flung at him.

"The mustangs do," he said. He strode past her and caught up to Dolly as she crossed in front of the cabin. He heard Prudence half running after him.

"Can I ride him?" Dolly asked Fargo, nodding to the brown gelding.

"Yes," Prudence cut in. "The swelling's gone. I can see that from here. You can ride right out of here."

Dolly turned to the slender, stiff-backed form, met Prudence's anger with a kind of edged pity. "Jesus, you've got it bad, honey," she said.

"I don't have anything bad. It's a matter of behavior, good taste, respect, maybe even honesty," Prudence said. "You just wouldn't understand."

"I understand, honey. You're the one who doesn't," Dolly said as she moved toward the horse.

Fargo, his eyes on Prudence, reached out to halt Dolly. "She's not going, not in midafternoon. Egan's scouting party might spot her," he said.

Prudence's face stayed cast in ice. "They won't see her. She can circle instead of going straight. She knows what to do. She's ridden it often enough," Prudence bit out.

"No, it's too risky," Fargo said firmly.

Dolly took his hand from her arm. "I'll be all right. I don't stay where I'm not wanted," she said.

Fargo's eyes stayed hard on Prudence. "Dammit, she'll at least stay till dark," he said.

"She can wait for dark over the ridge, down in the timber, anywhere, but not here," Prudence snapped back, turning her eyes away from Fargo's anger, her jaw staying set.

Dolly's hand touched his arm. "Forget it. I'll be all right," she said. She walked on, and he went with her to halt beside the horse, gave her a hand into the saddle. Dolly's eyes held quiet satisfaction in them as she looked down at him. "It was still something special," she said. "I'll be waiting in Threadneedle."

"I'll try," he told her. "Be careful on the way back." She nodded and moved the horse into a walk, waved a hand back as she disappeared into the timber. Fargo turned to the cabin, his eyes blue agate. Prudence leaned against the outside wall, the rifle against the cabin. He halted in front of her, and there was no give in her face, only an angry seething that turned her wild beauty hard-edged. "I never figured you being that rotten bitchy," Fargo said.

"Go after her, then, if you're so taken with her. I told you, I don't need you," Prudence threw back, anger and defensiveness in her voice.

"I'm not taken with her. Hell, we only just met, but she wanted it, and I never turn down a good offer and it was real good, but that's all there was. As for you, you don't know what you need and that's the only excuse you've got for being so goddamn bitchy," Fargo said.

Prudence met the anger in his blue agate eyes, held steady with her own defiance, and then looked away. She reached for the rifle. "I'm going to get us something to eat for dinner," she said. Fargo glanced up at the late-afternoon sky. There wasn't enough day left to ride up to the high plateau and scout the terrain over the passageway. It'd have to wait for morning, he decided.

"I'll get us dinner. You pick some scallions. I saw them growing over yonder," he growled. He took the big Sharps from its saddle holster and stalked from the cabin. In the surrounding woodland the light had already grown dim. He halted, waited, listening, caught the sudden flurry of sound, spun as the hare leaped into view. He fired, too quickly, missed, and swore at himself. His anger at Prudence still pushed at him, and Dolly kept intruding on his thoughts. He forced both down and moved through the woods. The hare had vanished and seemed to have no companions. He stalked the woods for almost an hour, and dark began to seep heavily through the trees. He started a long circle back toward the cabin, moving slowly, eyes probing the near darkness. But he was ready when the brush rabbit broke into the open. The Sharps exploded on target this time, and Fargo hurried back to the cabin with dinner in hand as night came down to curtain the land.

He tossed the rabbit on the table, skinned it quickly and deftly while Prudence boiled the water in the black kettle, flavored it with wild herbs, scallions, and pieces of the potatolike tuber called groundnut. The rabbit cooked quickly over the hot fire, and Fargo stood in the doorway, the night warm, moist air lying like a fine blanket in the air, and he felt the edginess stab at him and refuse to be pushed aside. When Prudence finally called, he went inside. He ate a dozen mouthfuls and suddenly pushed back from the table. "Now what?" Prudence asked, breaking the silence.

"I shouldn't have let her go," Fargo said through tight lips. "I feel it in my bones."

"She's perfectly all right," Prudence muttered.

"You want to keep telling yourself that," Fargo said. "I've got a bad feeling and I'm going to find out. I'm just sorry I let her give in to your goddamn rotten bitchiness."

"You're blaming me if anything's happened to her," Prudence said.

"Got any other candidates?" Fargo tossed back as he strode from the cabin. She followed him out as he saddled the Ovaro, watched him finish the task and swing onto the horse.

"I don't want anything to happen to her," she said. "I wouldn't want that."

Fargo looked at her. She wasn't contrite, but the anger had gone from her. "No, I'll give you that much," he said. "But if it's turned bad you can thank yourself for it." He spurred the pinto forward, left her watching him disappear into the night. He rode through the timber in the pale light of a three-quarter moon that barely filtered into the heavy woods. Dolly had some two hours' start, three with the time he could make in the dark. He followed the mountain slopes downward by instinct as much as by trail in the near dark, came upon a clear slope, and sent the Ovaro into a full-out gallop to make up time. Another timber stand came up before him, and he slowed once more, threaded his way through the denseness with tight-lipped impatience.

He had come halfway down the mountain when he halted in a thick stand of cottonwoods and alders. A sound drifted through the near dark, low, rising and falling, a half moan, half sob, became a woman's voice, and Fargo moved the pinto forward, edged to the right, followed the sound. It grew closer though hardly stronger, and he halted as he caught a pinpoint of light through the trees. Dismounting, he moved forward on foot, leading the pinto, then left the horse as the pinpoint of light became a very small fire. The half sob, half moan continued, interrupted by a shuddered crying, and Fargo crept forward until he was within a yard of the fire. Two figures came into view, seated near each other, two men, and Fargo's eyes moved to the side to see Dolly naked on the ground, clothes scattered beside her. Her full-fleshed body was covered with red welts, some trickling blood, one side of her face black and blue. One large breast bore ugly burn marks on the underside.

110

She cried out again as he let his eyes hold on her bruised, bleeding body. They hadn't tied her, he saw. There was no need, he noted grimly. She was too battered and abused to run off.

His eyes turned to the two men, and he felt the rage spiraling inside himself. Both were awake, grunting words at each other, completely unaware of the silent figure moving toward them. Fargo rose as he reached the edge of the spot, the Colt in his hand. He shot a quick glance at Dolly's sobbing form, stepped forward, and brought the Colt down alongside the nearest man's head. The figure toppled sideways with a gasp of pain, and the second man whirled, reached for his gun, but Fargo swung the Colt backhanded. It smashed across the man's face, and he fell backward with a small shower of teeth spitting from his mouth.

Fargo yanked the gun from the first one's holster, flung it aside, stepped forward, and did the same with the second one's gun. He heard them both land on the ground behind him, near where Dolly lay. The first man half rose, the side of his face streaming blood, a shock of thick black hair falling half over his forehead. He had started to push to his feet when Fargo's kick caught him in the pit of the stomach, and he fell backward doubled over, a guttural gasp of pain squeezing from his mouth. "That one's for Dolly," Fargo muttered as he moved toward the second man, who had risen to one knee, his mouth and chin a smear of red. The man dived for a length of half-burned wood, and Fargo's knee caught him alongside the shoulder. He sprawled sideways, had just hit the ground when Fargo smashed the Colt across his face again, this time across the bridge of his nose. The crack of bone was almost drowned out by the man's cry of pain as he fell, rolled, both hands in front of his face.

The first one still lay doubled up on the ground,

groaning softly, and Fargo stepped to where Dolly lay, half-lifted her in his arms. "No, no more, oh, God, please . . ." Dolly half-cried.

"Easy, you're all right. It's me, girl," Fargo said.

Her eyes came open and she stared at him. "Oh, Jesus," she breathed and fell against him, her body shuddering.

"It's all right, it's over," he murmured as he looked across at the two figures. She clung until she pushed back, her face still flooded with gratitude. He pulled her clothes to her. "Can you put these on?" he asked, and she nodded. One of the two figures stirred, and Fargo rose, left Dolly, and was beside the figure in one long stride. It was the one with the thick black hair. He looked up at Fargo with one hand still clutching his stomach. "There were five of you. Where are the others?" Fargo asked.

"Gone back," the man said, his voice a rasping wheeze.

"They're lucky," Fargo hissed. He glanced at Dolly. She had the blouse on, rested on her knees as she tugged the skirt on. Fargo stepped around the man to where the one with the smashed face had started to pull himself to his feet. "Over there with him," Fargo ordered, and the man stumbled forward to sink down beside the other, his face a smear of dripping red. Fargo stared down at the two men with his eyes cold as blue ice. "You stinking bastards. You tortured her to make her talk," he said.

"Not me," the one mumbled.

"Bullshit," Fargo said. "You all took turns. I know your kind. I'm going to tie you and leave you here for wolf bait."

The one with the red smear instead of a face started to protest. He might have gotten his mouth open. It was hard to tell, when the two shots exploded the night and Fargo saw both figures half leap, jerk crazily, and topple backward. He spun to see Dolly, the gun held with both hands. She fired again, two more shots, and the figures on the ground jerked convulsively as the bullets slammed into them. She'd emptied the gun as Fargo reached her, pried it from her hands. "Bastards. Goddamn bastards," she sobbed as he held her against him until she stopped shuddering. He gazed over her head to the two bullet-riddled forms on the ground. Dolly had taken justice into her own hands, and he wasn't one to judge her.

"Think you can ride?" he asked gently.

"I'll ride," she breathed. "Goddamn, I'll ride."

"Wait here," he said, lowering her to the ground. He brought the pinto back and took her horse from where they'd tied it. He pulled her into the saddle with him, sat her in front of him, and held the brown gelding's reins with one hand. He moved the pinto in a slow walk through the dark, back up the mountain trails. Dolly leaned heavily against him and cried out in pain too often.

"Fargo," she breathed as they rode. "I told them."

"Told them what?" he asked.

"The way to Prudence's cabin and the plateau," she said. "That's what they wanted. I'm sorry. I haven't the guts for taking a lot of pain. Jesus, I'm sorry."

He pressed a finger to her lips, reached his hand around to do so. "We are what we are," he said. "I'd say you held out long enough. Just sit back and rest." She laid her head back against his chest and rode with him in fits of sleep. It was still dark when he reached the cabin, though morning nudged the high peaks. Prudence ran out at once, rifle in hand, and her eyes grew round as she saw Dolly. She set the gun down and helped him ease the girl to the ground and into the house. She winced when he pulled Dolly's clothes from her as she lay on the bed. He saw her turn her face away, and he took her chin in his hand, brought her face back to the

113

bed, and her eyes were round with her own pain now. "No hiding place," he growled. Prudence nodded slowly, and her eyes moved across Dolly's scarred and bruised body. She turned and fetched the ointment. He reached for it and she pushed him aside.

"I'll do it," she said. "Please?" He nodded and stepped back. He went outside to see the day slide over the mountain tops, leaned against the cabin until Prudence emerged to stand beside him, her high-planed face drawn with its own pain. "She's sleeping," she murmured.

"Best thing for her," he said. "She told them the way up to the plateau. They tortured it out of her."

Prudence nodded, her face held very still. "It wouldn't have happened if I hadn't insisted she go then," Prudence said evenly, no self-pity in her voice, and he gave her credit for that.

"Wrong or not, it's done. No good in looking back now," he said.

"Maybe not much good in looking forward, either," she said.

He shrugged. "I'll stretch out a few hours and then ride some. We can talk more afterward," he said.

"One thing now," she said and turned to him, her eyes grave. "I'll try to save the horses, whatever it costs me. I'll understand if you decide to bow out along the way. I'm grateful for what you've done. I'm not asking anything more, not now."

"Why not now?" he questioned.

"It's all changed, not for the good. I counted on more time. I won't have that now. They'll be here in a matter of days, I'd guess," she said.

He turned from her and took his bedroll. "You tend to Dolly. We'll talk later," he said. He left her and found a shaded place, lay down on the blanket, and slept, woke when his inner alarm prodded him. He washed beside

114

the well and had just finished when Prudence stepped from the house.

"She's sleeping again," Prudence said, anticipating his question. "She woke before and I gave her some good broth. She'll be feeling better come night."

"Good," Fargo commented.

"I took a long look at her wounds. Most will go away in time," Prudence said.

"Most?" he echoed.

Prudence bit down on her lips. "Not the burn marks, damn their souls. That's the kind of men Jack Egan hires, men like himself who don't care about anything or anybody."

"They paid for it," Fargo said as he pulled himself onto the pinto. "I'll be back later," he said and rode quickly, moving up the steep slopes to the high plateau. He halted there and let his eyes scan the edges, move across the wild Arabians that rippled across the flat land. He searched for the ebony stallion and failed to see him, turned and rode to the sheer rock at the end of the plateau and the narrow passage through it. He rode the passageway to emerge at the other side and turned the pinto to climb the steep ground that led to the top of the rock. He carefully moved the pinto along the edge of the defile, made his way from one end to the other and back again. He halted as he scanned the rocks that covered the top of the area, his lips pursed as he let thoughts evolve themselves in his mind. Dolly's estimate circled his thoughts, fifteen, perhaps twenty men, and only one thought held on, a single countermove that could work. He let a wry sound escape his lips. If he could put it into place. If he could find time and the way.

He dismounted, moved among the large rocks that dotted the top of the land, edging passageway below. He walked back and forth, halting at each boulder, dwarfed by most, and he scanned the earth beside each, measured distances with his eyes, surveyed each a half-dozen times. Finally, as dusk began to tint the air, he remounted and made his way carefully down the steep slope to the exit of the passageway below. He rode back through the defile and emerged onto the high plateau, paused again to search the wild horses as they moved, instantly restless at the presence of an intruder. This time he spied the magnificent black stallion, standing apart from the others, ears flicking, the classic Arabian profile raised high, every sense alert. Fargo took another moment to enjoy the beauty of the great horse and then rode on along the edge of the plateau and down the timbered slopes until he reached the cabin.

He entered to see Dolly sitting up, a shawl around her shoulders. Her bruised face had turned purplish along one side of her cheek and jaw, but she managed a smile. "Been waiting for you to get back," she said. "Prudence is out scouting the low ridges."

"How do you feel?" he asked.

"Sore but a lot better. That salve of Prudence's is great stuff," Dolly said. He nodded agreement and noted a brace of quail on a spit over the fire, almost done roasting. Dolly's hand reached out to him. "Thanks for coming after me. I wouldn't be here if it weren't for you."

"Forget it. You're here, and that part's done with," Fargo said.

"But the rest is just about to begin," Dolly said, and he held grimness in his face as he agreed. "Convince her to run," Dolly said. "She can't stand off the force Egan's bringing."

"She won't run. She's too caught up with it," Fargo said. "It's not just having sympathy for the Arabians. It's not just ideals or principles. It's from inside. She's one with them. She feels as they do. It's an understanding of the heart, not the head."

Dolly studied him with narrowed eyes. "And you, Fargo?" she said. "You understand, too. It's inside you, too. You wouldn't be here otherwise."

His laugh held wry admission in it. "You've been around too much, Dolly. Maybe it's the one-quarter Cherokee in me," he said.

He turned as Prudence appeared in the doorway, rifle in hand, her eyes finding him beside Dolly at once, but he saw her soften the instant sharpness in her glance. "See anything?" he asked.

She shook her head as she set the rifle down. "Nothing. It's all quiet yet," she said. He helped her as she took the birds from the spit, used his throwing knife to carve. Dolly ate some and lay back on the bed.

"Sorry," she murmured. "I fade fast yet." She closed her eyes and was asleep before Fargo found words. He turned to Prudence as she finished eating.

"We'll talk outside," he said.

"I'll just clean up first," she said. He went outside into the warm night air, watched the moon approaching fullness, the scent of hemlock sweetening the air. Prudence came outside to stand beside him, her eyes moving along the dark outlines of the mountains, moonlight touching the planes of her face to give her a stark, spare beauty, her shirt resting lightly on small twin protrusions, tightened into a slender waist.

"Find us any answers?" she asked with grimness in her voice.

"A long shot, if we can make it work," he said.

"Tell me," she said.

"Telling's no good. I'll show you come morning so you can judge for yourself," he said. "Right now I need some sleep," he added as he felt his body remind him of the sleepless night before. His lips edged a tiny smile. "We're

117

sharing the floor tonight. Are we sharing a blanket, too?" he asked.

"You've brass asking that," Prudence flared at once. "I'm sorry about Dolly. I was wrong there, and I told you that, her, too. But I'm not taking back anything else I said."

"Good, because I'm not, either," he returned and strode into the darkness of the little cabin, only a few embers still glowing in the fireplace. He spread his blanket in a corner and was all but asleep when Prudence came in, heard her as she undressed quickly. He let sleep encircle him, welcomed its dark caress.

7

He saddled the horses in the early day as Prudence tended to Dolly and then came outside to join him. The new sun was already burning as he led the way up to the plateau, where Prudence paused to scan the mustangs, gesture to the shining ebony form standing high on a flat rock. She followed Fargo through the narrow passageway and up the steep, difficult climb to the top of the rock. He dismounted and faced her standing beside one of the boulders not far from the edge of the defile.

"We can't fight off twenty gunslingers in a running gunfight, and we can't hole up and stand them off. We've got to have an advantage. We've got to trap them," Fargo said.

"Just how do you figure to do that from up here?" Prudence questioned.

He patted the big boulder beside him and gestured to another a dozen yards away, each some ten feet in diameter. "With these," he said. "Egan's men will think they've boxed in the herd. It'll take a few minutes for them to realize that the mustangs are escaping through the passage. They'll race through after them. These two boulders, dropped at the right time, could seal off both ends of the passageway and trap Egan's force inside." He took Prudence by the arm and brought her to the edge of the defile where she could look down at the narrow passage below. "It wouldn't be a perfect seal, naturally. They could get out on foot, I'm sure, but it'd be enough to make them sitting ducks for riflefire from up here. We can do in damn near the whole lot of them while they're still figuring out what happened."

Prudence frowned down at the passageway below, turned back to Fargo. "Only one thing," she said. "There's no way we're going to do it. We can't push those two boulders to the edge here."

"We've three strong horses and enough lariat. I think we can do it," he said.

"And if we get them to the edge, what then?" she queried.

"They'll be on fulcrums, saplings we'll use as levers. A man can move a thousand times his weight with a fulcrum," Fargo said. "You just get your shoulder into it, push and lift, and they'll go over."

Prudence frowned at him in silence. "It's crazy," she murmured. "Unless we can make it work somehow."

"It's try or hightail it out of here and forget the mustangs," Fargo stabbed at her, saw the protest leap in her eyes at once. "There's no other way we can make a stand. I could see fighting off maybe ten, even a dozen, but not the force he's bringing with him."

"What do we do first?" she asked, the question her answer.

"You go back, look in on Dolly, and then bring her horse up here. Leave me your lariat, meanwhile," he said. Prudence climbed onto the chestnut and handed him the lariat, and he watched her negotiate the steep slope downward and gallop back through the passageway below. When she was out of sight he began to gather loose lengths of wood, breaking off saplings to add to the others. He positioned the lengths of wood near the top edge of the defile at both ends, laid down enough pieces at each end so at least two would stay in position. He began to circle the roundest boulder with the lariats, making three loops and tying each with a slip knot at the end. It was slow and frustrating work as the ropes slipped so often, but he'd finally finished the first boulder when Prudence returned, leading Dolly's gelding.

Fargo stepped back, let his arms rest a moment. "How is she?" he asked.

"Coming along amazingly well. She's a strong girl with a lot of drive," Prudence said. "Where do you want the horses placed?"

"Line them up close together," Fargo said as he took the end of the first length of lariat and looped it around the pinto's head and neck, drawing it tight around the point of the shoulder and bringing it up to make a loop over the withers. Prudence helped do the same with the other two horses, and finally Fargo stepped back and surveyed the finished result. It was not unlike a logger's rig. He stepped to the front of the three horses, gathered their reins in one hand. Prudence had positioned herself, and at a nod from Fargo she brought her palm down sharply on the chestnut's rump. He darted forward and the other two horses with him as Fargo yanked on the reins. The boulder rolled six inches, then two of the ropes slipped upward and came loose.

"Damn," Fargo swore and backed the horses. "Let them stay rigged. I think I can get the ropes lowered again without starting all over." Prudence held the three mounts in position as Fargo pulled on the ropes around the boulder, laboriously slid them down lower on the big rock until his fingers grew red and scraped. Finally he stepped back, returned to where Prudence waited, and took the reins from her. He signaled, and she slapped the chestnut again. The three horses moved together, pulled, and the boulder had rolled almost a foot when one of the knots gave way.

Fargo's oath rolled across the mountains. He retied the rope and drew the lariat lower on the rock. "Try and try again," he muttered as the horses pulled once more. The hitch on Dolly's horse slipped, and Fargo called a halt to redo it. The day was more than half over when it all came together on the sixth attempt. The horses pulled again, and with a ponderous, crunching motion, the boulder rolled and Fargo guided the horses along the edge of the passageway. He halted their forward motion when the rock rested over two long wooden poles on the ground. He untied the horses and stepped back, strode to the end of one of the long wooden poles. He took hold of the very end, lifted, and felt the boulder start to move. He quickly lowered the pole.

"It'll go over," he grunted. "Wonderful thing, the lever. One more to go." He walked, leading the horses, to the other end of the defile. The boulder he'd chosen for that end proved less troublesome, the surface covered with little outcroppings that caught the ropes and held them in place. It took only two attempts before it rolled to the edge of the defile and rested on the three wood levers Fargo had placed there. Once more, he tested the makeshift fulcrums and was satisfied. "There's only the waiting, now," he said as he unhitched the horses and mounted the Ovaro.

"We have to be up here before the Wild Shadow leads the herd through the passageway," Prudence said as they started down the steep slope.

"We'll be here," Fargo grunted. "Timing—and we can't do that till we see how it develops. Egan will reach the cabin, first. We won't be there then. We'll stay ahead of him and watch, wait, pick and choose when to make our move."

"You really think we can do it?" she asked.

He didn't answer quickly. "It'll be touch and go," he said finally. "And it'll all have to fall our way."

"If it doesn't?" she pressed.

"We're in trouble," he told her.

She rode the rest of the way in silence and halted when they reached the plateau. Her eyes swept the Arabians as they ran, frolicked, tossed manes and tails high. In her high-planed face he saw love and despair, and she finally rode on with her lips pressed hard onto each other. Night reached the cabin before they did, and Fargo stared in amazement at Dolly's figure in the doorway.

"You sure bounce back fast," he said.

"I've got reasons," she answered. "I can't be here when they come. I'll only be a burden to you. You'll have enough to do without me on your hands." Fargo didn't disagree. She deserved honesty. "I want to leave, now, tonight," she said, and her eyes found Prudence. "Isn't there some other way down from here?"

"The back of the mountain," Prudence said. "It's longer, and when you reach the foothills you've got to circle all the way around to get back to Threadneedle. But it'll avoid running into Egan. I can take you most of the way down, enough for you to go on alone."

"Let's go," Dolly said. "It'll hurt riding, but I'll stand it." Prudence turned back to her horse, pulled herself into the saddle. Fargo helped Dolly up onto the brown gelding and saw her wince. "I'll still be waiting in Threadneedle," she said to him and found a rueful smile to offer. He nodded, and his eyes met Prudence's as she turned the chestnut around, her jaw suddenly grown set. She rode on, and Dolly followed, both horses quickly swallowed up in the night. He unsaddled the pinto and corralled the horse, made a flame with a few twigs, and heated the rich broth he found in the house. He sipped the brew outside, the night hot, the air thick. He sat against the cabin and listened to the forest noises. A distant horned owl hooted its deep, hollow sound. He rose and went inside finally, satisfied there were no sounds foreign to the forest night.

He undressed and lay in the blackness of the cabin, the door open to let the night air circulate. He slept fitfully, woke at once as he heard Prudence returning, listened to her corral the chestnut. He saw her shadowed figure enter the cabin, become part of the darkness as she quickly undressed, and heard her sleep almost at once, the even sound of her breathing strangely loud in the little cabin. She was still asleep when he woke with the new day, and he realized it had been close to dawn when she'd returned. The dawn came in humid, and the blue-gray nightgown had ridden as she slept to reveal two slender but beautifully curved legs, smooth calves and small knees, the lower part of her thighs tight-skinned and graceful. He rose silently, took his things, and dressed outside.

She was still asleep when he finished saddling the pinto and rode into the timber, headed slowly downward through woods spattered by the new sun. He rode unhurriedly, a slow, steady pace down the mountainsides, halted as a clear slope opened up before him, scanned the far edge before crossing. Heavy woodland rose up again, but the trail was firm inside him now, and he moved the pinto easily through the forests. He had ridden down for a good part of the morning, almost to where he'd dispatched the two gunslingers that had seized Dolly, when his eye caught the movement of thick foliage below. He reined up, watched, traced the moving branches with his eyes, saw another area of foliage move to the left. He edged the pinto sideways into a thick glen of alder, waited, and the figures came into sight soon, moving through the trees below. Two groups, moving side by side, he noted, staying a few yards apart. He watched as the riders came into sight, disappeared through thick foliage, came into his view once more.

They were too far away to make out faces, but they were moving steadily, almost boldly, he noted. He drew the big Sharps from its saddle-case holster. He'd slow them down, let them know the taste of fear. He'd make them move with caution, look carefully with each step, probe, test, ride nervous. And give Prudence and himself another twelve hours perhaps. He lifted the big rifle to his shoulders, his gaze traveling down the long, smooth barrel and through the front sights. He picked out a rider at the edge of the nearest group, watched him disappear behind foliage, reappear again. Slowly, Fargo squeezed the trigger of the big Sharps. The sharp crack echoed, bounced from slope to slope, and he watched the figure throw both arms into the air and topple from the horse. The others became a blur of movement as they scattered in all directions, and he picked up the sound of curses and shouted commands.

He sat quietly as silence came to the mountainside, the rifle held across his lap. He half smiled as he scanned the foliage below, where everything had grown still and silent. Five minutes, he guessed, not much more. He counted seconds off silently to amuse himself, had reached just past the four-minute mark when he saw the trees move below, one first, then a line of them, and he sat waiting in absolute silence. Figures began to appear, some running on foot through the trees, retrieving horses, making their way back carefully. He watched a small knot of figures gathered, half hidden by foliage. Egan was holding a small conference, Fargo grunted. The knot of figures broke apart, and Fargo saw the riders begin to move forward again, more slowly now. "Not slowly enough," he muttered aloud as he raised the rifle again.

He chose a figure on the other side this time, a rider he could barely bring into his sights. He let the man move through a space between leaves, held careful aim, and once more gently squeezed the trigger of the heavy rifle. He watched through the sight as the rider seemed to be blown sideways from his saddle by a tremendous gust of wind, and once again the shot was a sharp, clear cracking noise in the mountains. One more, the others streaked and scattered for cover.

Fargo smiled as he slid the rifle into its long saddle holster. It was enough, he commented to himself. Now they'd move at a snail's pace. The added time he wanted was secure. He turned the Ovaro and started back up the mountain slopes, riding unhurriedly, silently. Only when he was firmly beyond earshot did he push the pinto into a canter. Prudence was outside the cabin, drying clothes on a sun-baked stone, when he rode up and dismounted. The question was in her eyes, and he nodded gravely.

"They're on the way. They'll be taking a little longer. I slowed them down some," he said. "And there are two less."

"When will they reach us?" she asked.

"Tomorrow, I'd guess," he said. "We'll pull out tonight and make camp up near the plateau where we can stay back and watch."

"As many as Dolly said?" she asked.

"As many," he answered and saw her face grow grave. He sat down, cleaned his Colt and did the same with the big Sharps, stayed relaxed as Prudence grew increasingly tense. Night began to descend, and he rose, stretched. "Get your gear," he said. "Travel light. Leave some clothes lying around and the corral door open."

"You want them to know we've run?" she frowned.

"Let them think we've taken off only a little while before. It'll give them a dose of false confidence," he said. She followed his instructions and brought the chestnut alongside him as he mounted up and began the slow climb to the high plateau. The moon had come full and bathed the land with its pale, eerie clarity. It was far past the midnight hour when he crested the slope and gazed across the plateau and felt the surprise flood over him. The plateau was empty save for a pair of coyotes that trotted across its openness, and he frowned at Prudence.

"They go into the mountain recesses at night," she said. "They come back down to the plateau in the morning." She shrugged. "I don't know why. They have their reasons."

He nodded. The patterns of wild things only seemed mysterious to man. There were always reasons. He turned the pinto and led the way back into the timber, moving higher on the land that edged the plateau, climbed until he reached a ridge thick with spicebush and elderberry under a cover of chestnut oak. The spot looked down on the plateau, afforded a clear view from end to end. "This will do us," he said as he dismounted, took down his bedroll. The night stayed hot, and he undressed to shorts and stretched out on the bedroll. He saw Prudence wait, watch him, her eyes move over the length of his hard-muscled frame, and then she went into the thick brush to undress. She came back with a sheet held around herself, sat down on her blanket, and rolled herself cocoon-like inside the sheet. He heard her voice after a few moments, a hushed sound.

"I'm afraid, Fargo," she said. "Something's going to go wrong. I feel it inside."

He wanted to dismiss her words as only nerves, tense imaginings, fears. He had no such premonitions. But he had seen the wild sensitivity that was inside her, that special intuitive thread only the wild and the very young possess, and he could dismiss nothing. He had only one answer to offer. "Then we'll have to make it go right," he said. She accepted the words in silence, and soon he heard the even sound of her breathing in sleep. He turned on his side, one hand resting atop the Colt, and slept.

Morning came with the air already hot, the earth sending small steamy wisps of vapor into the still air. He rose, stepped to the rear of the brush, and saw the sparkle of a mountain stream some hundred yards behind the brush. He heard Prudence wake, saw her pull herself to her feet holding the sheet around her, and he gestured to the stream beyond. "You first," he said. "We've plenty of time."

She took her things, and he watched her trudge upward toward the stream, disappear in the thick woodland. He turned his gaze down to the plateau below. It was still empty, and his eyes moved to the far end where the rock rose high and the narrow passageway stayed hidden inside the rock wall. It would work, he told himself. If things went their way it would work. He found himself thinking of Prudence's fearful premonition. He pushed it aside as she came back down through the trees, dressed, her face still wet and looking fresh as a morning glory, her shirt lightly resting on twin points, her slender figure moving with easy grace. He took his things, climbed to the stream, and washed quickly in the cool water. The grass was soft as a pillow near the stream, he noted, thick and luxurious growth supplied by underground moisture.

When he returned to the thick brush, Prudence sat with her knees drawn up, her face grave, and he sat down beside her. "Still afraid?" he asked, and she nodded. He sat back, let silence hold the morning. The sun had started to move higher in the sky when he saw the first of the mustangs appear, begin to drift down onto the plateau, race and kick their heels exuberantly. It was nearing the noon hour, he estimated, as others began to appear. Suddenly he felt Prudence stiffen beside him, and he followed her gaze to see the riders coming up along the far edge of the plateau. He picked out Jack Egan wearing a wide-brimmed Stetson, and beside him the hawk face of Humphrey Wills, the good mayor of Threadneedle. Humphrey Wills hoped to strike two blows in one, a chance at revenge and a chance to return to the marriage racket. Fargo made a harsh sound. Wills had given himself a third opportunity he didn't seem to realize—the chance to be dead.

Fargo watched Egan halt and saw the man's gaze move over the mustangs on the plateau. Egan understood at once, he saw, as the man called in his riders, gave orders, hands moving in quick, sharp motions. In moments, the riders scattered, raced upward along the mountain slopes. It was hardly more than minutes when the sound of shouts and gunfire reverberated through the mountains, and Fargo felt Prudence's hand close over his forearm as the wild horses began to race onto the plateau. They raced down from a dozen places, running in fright and panic to join the others already on the flatland. The gunfire continued, Egan's men riding up and down the mountainside, and more Arabians raced into view, galloping onto the plateau. The herd grew in size quickly, the horses taking comfort in being together, growing less panicked. The gunfire and shouting continued, and still more Arabians appeared, racing down from passes only they knew, joining the others on the plateau. Fargo felt Prudence's fingers digging hard into his arm.

"They're doing just what you said they'd do," he told her.

"I kept hoping maybe they wouldn't," she murmured, a catch in her voice.

"Patterns," he reminded her, and she nodded unhappily.

"Stay calm. Just watch and wait," he said soothingly

as Egan's men continued to run the ridges and slopes. Another dozen mustangs raced onto the plateau to join the others before the day wore to an end. Fargo shifted position in the thick brush, his leg touching Prudence's thigh, and he watched Egan's men return to the far end of the plateau. He saw Egan bark more orders, and the riders began to move again in the gathering dusk. They rode across the far end of the plateau as Egan positioned them in a more or less straight line. Though there was plenty of space between them, their presence would be enough to keep the mustangs boxed in the plateau.

"No surprises," Fargo said to Prudence. "He's behaving just as you figured he would, also." She made no reply, and he saw her eyes were peering at the mustangs in the fast-fading light, the horses moving back and forth in nervous restlessness. Fargo brought his gaze back to the far end of the plateau. He could still make out Jack Egan in the wide-brimmed Stetson, Humphrey Wills at his side. "Egan will wait till morning to move in on the herd," Fargo said. "He'll keep his men in place through the night, and come tomorrow he can begin his wholesale slaughter." Again, Prudence said nothing, her eyes still fixed on the horses across the plateau. "We'll make our move just before dawn," Fargo said.

"He's not there," he heard Prudence say, her voice low, tight, and he turned to her, frowned at her as she continued to stare out across the plateau. "The Wild Shadow, he's not there," she said, her voice a half-whisper.

Fargo's gaze swiveled to the herd at once, his eyes straining, able to see little more than milling horses as the dark descended. "Are you sure?" he questioned.

"I'm sure. I looked back and forth over the entire plateau. He's not there. I'd know it if he were. I'd feel it even if I didn't see him," Prudence said, and he was certain she was right.

130

"He didn't come down with the others," Fargo said. "He's up on the slopes someplace."

"Not far," Prudence said. "But he won't go through their line on his own." She halted, her eyes peering into the dark as the full moon began to rise over the ridge-line. She turned her gaze on the big man beside her, her face grave. "You know what it means?" she asked, and he said nothing, let her finish. "It means the others won't go through the passageway tomorrow. They'll just mill about and run in panic when the shooting starts. They'll be without a leader. They won't run. They'll race in circles and be slaughtered."

Fargo felt his mouth grow tight. She was too right. The herd would be lost without their leader. It was part of herd behavior. They needed a leader, and there wasn't time enough for a new one to emerge. Her words of fear had come true. It had gone wrong. Without the wild stallion to lead them there was nothing, except the blood-bath victory for Egan.

Fargo stared across the dark in silence and knew the fury of anger and frustration. And one more thing. He knew that inside the slender figure beside him there was the heartbreak of helplessness, all the caring and all the love gone for nothing. The full moon rose higher and painted the outline of the herd with its soft silver light. The animals moved back and forth on the plateau, still restless in the hot night air. Prudence's voice came to him as if from very far away, hardly more than a whisper. "I could bring him to the herd," she said.

"You could what?" Fargo frowned.

"Ride the Wild Shadow, ride him onto the plateau with the herd," she said, her voice still a whisper but an edge in it now. Fargo continued to stare at her. "He'd go past Egan's men if I were on him. I could get him to do it," she said.

Fargo's eyes rose to the round, full sphere in the sky,

and she followed his gaze. He heard the despair turn in her voice at once. "They'd see me," she said. "Under that moon they'd see me, probably when I tried to slip through on my own. They'd be sure to see me coming back through on the Wild Shadow." She paused, and the bitterness laced her voice again. "They'd see me and figure something was going on. There'd be no surprise left for us come morning," she murmured.

Fargo gazed at the full moon again, then frowned at Prudence as the thought leaped inside his head. "They wouldn't think anything if they saw only the stallion come through," he said.

"If they see him, and they will, they'll see me on him," Prudence said.

"Not if you were black as he, lying flat over his back," Fargo said and heard the excitement catching in his voice. "They'd see only a black stallion racing past them onto the plateau to join the others."

"How?" Prudence asked, and now he heard the hope catching at her.

"You made black as the night, from head to toe, every part of you," Fargo said. "No clothes to flap, rustle, make outlines. Just you, naked and black, as pitch-black as the Wild Shadow." Prudence's eyes stayed on him, round, questioning. "By the stream there's good black earth. I noticed it when I was there. I can use the water to make a paste of black mud that'll stick to you."

He saw her eyes shine with hope, and the hesitation hold it back. "That's right," he guessed. "Naked, made black from head to toe. There's no other way. Clothes, any clothes, tear, blow in the wind, make outlines. You've got to be nothing but a black shadow."

Her eyes stayed on him, her face grave. "Let's go," she said quietly, turning and striding up the hill toward the stream. When they reached the mountain stream, a faint blue thread under the moon, he knelt down and began to tear up the earth near the bank. He scooped up water and made a paste thin enough to stay on and thick enough to cover. He looked up to see her standing stiffly.

"Get your clothes off," he said gruffly as he continued making the mud paste. She turned her back to him and began to undress. He watched her step out of her half-slip, the last garment on her, stand very straight with her back to him. He smiled inwardly as he took the moment to appreciate the loveliness of her, the slender, straight figure, the narrow waist, her rear flat and firm, her legs long and slender. "Over here," he said quietly and watched her turn, start toward him, and he saw her eyes were shut tightly. She halted in front of him, wide, strong shoulders, the modest breasts not all that modest suddenly, long, nicely rounded cups with tiny pink tips in the center of equally small dust-pink circles. An unexpected little bulge of belly below the narrow waist was an almost out-of-character sensuous note, and below it, a small but very thick, dense triangle, and long, slender thighs below that. Prudence Thorpe had one of those bodies more beautiful naked than clothed, the wildness inside her reflected in the spare litheness of her willow-rod body. He took her hand, drew her down onto her knees, and she kept her eyes shut.

He began to put the mud paste over her, the feel of the concoction coming between himself and her. He did her face first, included the tops of her closed eyelids, moved down along the slender neck, across her shoulders, arms. When he began to cover her breasts, his fingers trailing the mud paste across the tiny nipples, he heard the sharp intake of her breath, the little tremor run along her skin. "It's better without the mud," he commented softly and drew no reply. He moved down over her waist, patted, smoothed, covered every inch of her skin with the mud, went down to her belly. He took two handfuls of the mud-paste and began to smooth it

133

onto her legs, his hand pushing over the inside of her thighs. Her eyes snapped open and she reached down, caught his wrist.

"I'll do that part," she said firmly, and he pressed the mud into her hands. He brought her another handful as she rubbed the black paste over the inside of her thighs, up to the dark triangle, drew her hand away from the tiny rise of the pubic mound.

"Everything," he snapped.

"All right, you don't have to watch," she hissed. He turned away and fashioned more mud paste. She was standing when he finished, and he examined her, nodded approval. She turned for him to do her back, and he worked quickly but thoroughly, finally stepped away and circled her. He had covered every inch of her, from eyelids to the bottoms of her feet, and he was satisfied. She was hardly visible when he moved but a few feet away.

"Ready?" he asked.

"Ready," she said, and he began to descend the slope with her, walking slowly. They reached the edge of the plateau, and he walked alongside her in silence, more than halfway around the edge until they began to draw near to the far end where Egan and his men had made their loose line.

"Go out on the plateau and through the line at the far end," he said, and she nodded. "The stallion—how do you figure to find him?" he asked.

"He'll find me," she said simply.

"Good luck," he said. "Ride the Wild Shadow."

She nodded, turned from him, and he watched her break into a trot. He lost sight of her in moments, even in the full moon's light, and he was satisfied with that much. It was a good omen, he muttered inwardly as he moved back along the edge of the plateau. He wasted no energy hurrying. There was no need, and when he reached the thick brush of the ridge above the plateau, he settled down, lay back, and half-closed his eyes. He followed Prudence in his mind, traced her movements as though he could see her, drawing on what he had come to learn about this unusual, wild-in-heart girl. His pictures of the mind were not far from the mark.

The round moon drew a silvery brush across the herd of wild horses, and the magnificent animals watched, ears standing up, listened, moved back as the figure trotted through their ranks, a strange, black shadow. The silent figure trotted on soft, shoeless steps, moved quickly toward the far end of the plateau, and the moon lighted one of Egan's men on his horse, another figure some fifty yards distant. The figure moved forward in between the two horsemen, past the end of the plateau and into the foliage, unseen, unheard, a black wraith.

Prudence turned when she reached the foliage, climbed sharply up the slope to emerge where the timber grew sparse. She came to a stretch covered only by spicebush, and she halted, stood absolutely still. She was perspiring in the hot night air, the scent of her filtering through the mud paste covering her body. She waited, stood absolutely still, and then she heard the sound, powerful hoofbeats striking hard on the ground, and suddenly the great form appeared, a black shape racing down the slope. The stallion continued to bear down on her at a full gallop, skidded to a halt in a half-circle, the sensitive profile raised high, nostrils flared wide as he drew in scents. She spoke, sounds more than words, murmurings he had come to know, and the stallion pawed the ground, moved to her side, tossed the magnificent head high. Prudence laid her hands against him, let him feel her touch once again, then grasped hold of the full, jet mane and pulled herself onto his back. He reared, came down, and raced down the slope at once, and Prudence felt the soaring, driving power of him as he thundered along the ground and yet hardly seemed to touch earth.

He raced through the wooded part of the slope to emerge at the edge of the plateau. The stallion saw one of Egan's men in the distance, sensed the others, and Prudence felt him begin to slow. She leaned forward, murmured sounds, stroked the mighty neck muscles, drew her knees tight against the massive ribs. The stallion picked up speed, charged forward, and she stayed against his neck, pulled her legs up, and flattened herself along the broad ebony neck. Egan's man heard the thundering hooves. He leaned forward in his saddle, peered into the dark, frowned as he searched the night, and suddenly he glimpsed a great black form streaking across the flatland. The ebony form seemed hardly to touch the ground and disappeared into the moon-touched night, a wild shadow.

Fargo sat up abruptly. She had made it back. The knowing flooded through him, his own inner being not untouched by the wild senses. He pushed himself to his feet and began to trot down the slope in his long, loping stride until he reached the plateau. He halted, peered out at the herd. He picked out the dark shape that moved from the others, came nearer, halted, a moving shadow, and the shadow suddenly backed, vanished. Fargo waited, eyes straining into the dark, and suddenly the moonlight touched a figure moving toward him. He ran forward, suddenly afraid the shape might vanish, his eyes playing tricks on him. But it remained, became more than a shadow. He reached out and she came against him, her breath drawn out in long sighs.

"It's done. He's here," she whispered, in her voice relief mingled with a kind of awe. "It was like flying," she breathed. "As though we never touched ground."

She stayed against him, and he felt the heat from her.

"We've got to get that mud off you fast," he said. "Your body temperature's going up too fast." He took her hand, began to lope up the slope, pushing through brush until he reached the stream. He pushed her into the water, held her face down for a moment, pulled her up and clawed the mud from her, felt the rest begin to slip away. He sat her in the water and doused her with water as he used his hands to scrape away the mud paste. It began to come loose in large globs, and Prudence pushed more of it from her legs and abdomen. He lifted her from the water after a few minutes, put her down on the soft carpet of grass, and rubbed the remaining traces of the mud paste from her. His palms came around from her back to rub gently across her breasts, sliding away traces of the mud still there.

"No, I'll do it," she breathed, but he rubbed his hand slowly over the tiny pink tips, and he heard her little gasp. Her hands came up, closed around his wrists, but his palm had curled under one breast, cupping the soft mound. He could feel her skin now, smoothly firm. "No," she breathed as he rubbed his thumb over the little pink tip. He leaned forward, found her lips with his mouth, pressed, let his tongue dart forward, and her mouth opened, stayed open. Her hand let go of his wrist, and he felt her arms come up to encircle his neck. A shuddering tremor rushed through her, and she arched back, pulled him with her.

"Fargo . . . oh . . . oh, God . . . yes, yes, yes," she breathed. The shudder came to course through her again, and suddenly she pulled from his mouth, stared at him for a moment, then pushed her lips over his, a hungering, devouring kiss. He felt himself suddenly clasped as if in a vise as her legs came up, clapped around his hips. She flung her head back, and she half screamed at him. "Go on, go on, yes . . . oh, yes." She began to thrash from side to side, her body suddenly a wild, leaping serpent.

Her hands pulled his face down to her breasts, and he closed his mouth around one, and she screamed in pleasure. He let his lips pull on the tiny pink tips, suck them up into tiny little erect mounds. "Ah . . . aaaiiii . . . aaiiieeee . . ." she screamed, and she thrust her pelvis upward for him, urging, offering, as her arms fell against the grass, her hands little fists pounding the earth, then his ribs, and there was no holding back, no denying her explosion of wild wanting.

He slid into her opened portal and felt its tightness, heard her cry out in pain. "Ow . . . ow . . . go on, go on . . . oh, yes, yes . . . go on." He had hesitated, and she thrust herself upward over him, her hips quivering, her pubic mound almost leaping upward with each thrust of her hips. He pressed deeper, moved inside her, back and forth, feeling his responses catch hold with her urgings. Her head rolled from side to side, and she cried out in ecstasy and release. "More, more . . . oh, please, more," she gasped, and he began to ram into her as deeply as his pulsating, magnificent maleness could go. "Iiiiieee . . . aaaiiiii . . . aaaah," she screamed and demanded more with her quivering, shuddering body. Her legs clasped and unclasped around him, each time a harsh, urging blow of flesh against flesh, and even as she half screamed, half cried, she pushed her breasts into his mouth, wanted every part of her immersed in pleasure. He felt himself lifted, brought down, lifted again as her abandon increased. "Please, please . . . oh, yes, oh more, more," she cried out, and she seemed a thing of absolute insatiable wanting, the wildness inside her all released in the demands of wanting.

He felt himself swelling inside her, and suddenly her cries halted, an almost soundless gasp of air pushing from her throat. He saw her neck arch backward, her head press back against the grass, and she exploded with him, crying out guttural gasps as she throbbed around his organ, muscles contracting, loosening, contracting again, and her head fell from side to side, her hands convulsively opening and closing against him. "Ah . . . ah . . . ah . . ." the gasped sounds came, matching her ecstatic contractions, and he saw her eyes were open, staring at him in a kind of disbelief, an incomprehension of the total depths of her pleasure.

She fell back on the grass with a shuddered sigh, pulled his head against her breasts and held him there until, finally, her legs fell open to give up the throbbing trophy she had claimed. She met his eyes as he lay half over her, one hand cupping a firm-soft breast. "I knew it would be like this one day," she murmured. "It had to be. I knew it." She paused, reflected silently for a long moment. "It had to be someone like you," she said. "Someone who understands the wild things, too."

He smiled at her, let a thought of his own hold inside him. But she caught his moment at once. "Tell me," she said. "You're thinking something."

"I was thinking that you rode one Wild Shadow tonight and I rode another," he said.

Her smile was suddenly full of sly satisfaction. "The morning's a long time away yet," she said.

"Long enough," he agreed and saw the sage-green eyes grow cloudy and the shudder course through her slender body again. Her arms came around his neck with harsh urgency, and her wiry, lithe form half twisted, came around to come over him. Her hand reached down for him, found his organ lifting in instant response. She held him and trembled, and he felt the pleasure of the moment racing through her, running up her arm, down into her breasts as they quivered against him, down to the pulsating little mound she lowered over him.

"Please," she said, but the word was almost screamed, a demand, not a request, and the wildness seized her again as he obeyed, lifted, turned her roughly on her back and pushed into her. Her cry was made of fervent welcome and her hands clutched at him again. He gave her all she demanded and more, and finally she lay beside him, her body wet with perspiration as was his. He held her head in the crook of his arm as he let the warm air dry his body. She slept without another word to him, lithe young body and the sweet, firm breasts suddenly made of young girl beauty. He closed his eyes, reluctantly but aware that he'd perhaps only an hour or two till dawn.

8

The warm wind of dawn woke him, and he rose, shaking Prudence into wakefulness. "Dress. Seconds count now," he said gruffly. She rubbed sleep from her eyes and pulled on clothes, ran to the stream to freshen up, and hurried back to join him where he waited on the pinto. She followed as he led the way down to the edge of the plateau and began to move toward the other end, staying in the tree line to come onto the plateau itself only when the sheer rock forced the move. He reached the passageway in the rock and reined up as he saw Prudence had halted, her eyes looking back across the flatland to the mustangs, her face suddenly tight.

"Prudence," he called softly, and she turned to follow. He took the passageway at a full gallop, slowed only when he came out at the other end and turned to send the pinto up the precipitous path to the top of the rocks. At the top, he dismounted at once and knelt down beside the boulder poised at the edge of the defile. Prudence came to kneel beside him, her eyes following his gaze down at the passageway below. From where they waited, they could only see along half of the defile. Fargo patted the boulder with his hand. "It won't seal off the passage completely, but they'll have to scramble on foot to get out," he said. "Those left to scramble," he added.

Prudence was silent, her eyes fixed as far along the passageway as she could see. "Nothing to say about last night?" she asked, not taking her gaze from the passage way below.

"I enjoyed it," he answered.

"Nothing about how you knew all along?" she pressed.

"No need to," he said. The first shot cut off further talk, and a volley of pistol shots followed, all still distant. Egan was starting to drive the herd down to the end of the plateau, where his men could pour fire into them as they concentrated in one place. Fargo saw a small cloud of dust rise slowly into the air. "They're running," he murmured. "You take the second lever. I'll take the first," he said to Prudence, and she nodded understanding. The roar of thundering hoofbeats grew louder, as did the sound of Egan's men firing into the air. He saw Prudence stiffen as she caught movement along the passage.

"They're coming through. He's leading them," she said, and Fargo saw the ebony stallion appear in the passageway below, running full out with another horse on his heels. He glanced at Prudence, saw the wild shining in her eyes. Fargo returned his gaze to the bottom of the defile. The mustangs followed close on the heels of the big stallion, taking the narrow defile singly or in uneven pairs. The shots had stopped, and Fargo could almost hear Egan's furious curses as by now he realized what had happened. Fargo rose as the last of the mustangs came into view, raced past and into the hill country beyond.

"Get over to your lever," he ordered, and Prudence ran to the second of the two long poles. Fargo waited, saw Egan appear, Humphrey Wills close behind him and the others following. He counted off seconds as the men raced for the end of the passageway, held for a moment longer, and then leaped to the first of the two poles. "Now," he hissed and began to lift his lever, felt Prudence's efforts helping. The boulder moved, rolled, and Fargo lifted higher. The boulder rolled over the edge with what seemed infuriating slowness, and Fargo dropped the length of wood, didn't wait to watch over the edge. He leaped onto the Ovaro, beckoned to Prudence, and heard the rumbling crash as the boulder struck bottom. The sound of shouts and curses spiraled up from the bottom of the passageway as Fargo raced the pinto to the other boulder. He was on the ground before the horse came to a halt, lifting the long lever under the other boulder. Prudence came up to do her part, her shoulder fitting in beside his. He felt the boulder move, roll an inch, move again. It teetered on the edge for a moment and then plunged over, hitting the steep side of the defile as it plummeted.

The crash resounded, loud in the narrow confines of the defile, and Fargo had the big Sharps out of its holster, flung a glance at Prudence as she strode to the chestnut and got her rifle. He dropped to one knee at the edge of the passageway, his eyes sweeping the riders below as they raced back and forth between the two blocked ends of the cut. He spotted Humphrey Wills reining to a halt beside Egan. Their voices carried upward clearly, the narrow, stone-walled passage a natural sound chamber.

"No goddamn accident," Wills said. "Sonofabitches."

"You called it, no goddamn accident," Fargo agreed through lips that hardly moved. Two more riders raced back from the other end of the passage. The big Sharps fired, two quick shots, and the men catapulted from their horses. Fargo saw Egan duck, slide from the saddle, look up, but others were racing to the center of the passage, drawn by the shots. The rifle exploded again, a volley of shots, and three more men toppled. Fargo reloaded, frowned at Prudence as she peered down, the rifle at her shoulder. "Shoot, goddammit," he yelled. He saw her face tighten and she pulled the trigger, a slow volley. But he saw three more figures fall, and now the men below were racing back and forth, trying to find a place to take cover, a few dropping to the ground, attempting to flatten themselves against the stone sides of the passage. But there was no hiding place, and Fargo laid down a barrage of fire, saw figures toppling in all directions, shouts, curses, cries of pain all mingling to spiral upward. He saw Egan staying behind his horse, moving back and forth, using the animal as a shield, and decided not to risk a shot at the man. He chose two others who were racing for the far end of the passage, brought them both down.

Some had dropped to one knee and tried firing up at the top of the rocks, but their shots were wild, passing harmlessly into the air. Fargo caught a man trying to run on foot. His shot slammed into its target, and the figure, racing forward, seemed to do a kind of stumbling dance, momentum carrying it on until it pitched face first into the stone wall of the passage, slid to the ground with head twisted up and back grotesquely. Fargo reloaded, started to fire another volley at the panicked figures below. Egan had taken refuge against the near wall behind his horse. Fargo's first shots brought down two more running figures.

"No more," he heard the voice call. "That's enough."

His head lifted from the rifle, and he stared at Prudence. She had stepped back from the edge, the rifle in her hands, her eyes dark with pain. "What'd you say?" he frowned.

"No more shooting," she repeated.

Fargo's frown deepened. "Hell, there's at least another half-dozen left besides Egan and that bastard Wills," he said. He turned his eyes to the rifle and fired again, saw his target spin, fall, one hand clutching his shoulder. The man's scream of pain echoed upward.

"No. Stop it," Prudence shouted.

Fargo turned to her again, disbelief in his stare. "What the hell for?" he barked.

"They're helpless. They're just sitting ducks," she said.

"Jesus, that was the idea," he countered.

"No more, now. It's just killing, slaughter," she said.

"What the hell's wrong with you?" Fargo threw back angrily. "You've got that short a memory. They were going to just slaughter all your Arabians."

She nodded. "I know. I'm not forgetting. But we've won, now," she said.

"Hell we have. They came looking for slaughter and they've found it," he bit out. He turned back to the barrel of the big Sharps and fired two shots down into the passageway. One missed, the other didn't, and he heard the man scream out in pain as the heavy rifle slug shattered the bone of his calf. The rifle exploded alongside him and he fell back as the shot sent a shower of rock fragments into the air a scant six inches from his head. From his back, he stared up at Prudence as she held the rifle on him. "You crazy?" he said in disbelief.

"I told you no more. It's enough," she said as he pushed himself to a sitting position. "We've won. They're helpless," she said.

He flung fury at her with his glare. "You and that goddamn sensitivity of yours. Don't you ever learn?" he said.

"I'll prove it to you," she said.

"You'll prove nothing. Stop wasting valuable time. I'm not for letting one damn gunslinger crawl out," Fargo insisted.

"Then you can put that rifle down," she said. "Your Colt, too."

"Goddamn, you went along with this," he said.

"I know, and I guess I didn't realize what it'd be like, just slaughtering them," she conceded. "We've done enough. They're through. Put your guns down or promise you won't shoot anymore."

He stared at her, saw the stubborn conviction in her face, her reasons once again not from the head but the heart, and he swore silently at those too vulnerable for their own good.

"No promises, but I'll hold back till you've done your proving," he said.

She lowered the rifle. "Fair enough," she said. He got to his feet as she moved to the edge of the defile, knelt on one knee, and looked down at the narrow passageway liberally littered with bodies. "Jack Egan, you hear me down there?" she called. Fargo lowered himself beside her. He saw the top of the wide-brimmed Stetson behind the horse now positioned against the opposite wall. His eyes swept the passageway, spotted Wills crouched to the left, another five figures edging their way behind their horses. The rest of the passageway held no movement. "Do you hear me?" Prudence called again.

"I hear you," Egan's voice came drifting up.

"You're trapped. You're finished," Prudence said. "Give up and there'll be no more killing."

"You talking for that big bastard, too?" Fargo heard Egan call.

Prudence shot Fargo a quick glance. "Yes, I'm talking for us both. Give up, put down your guns, and there'll be no more killing. You can go. All I want is a promise you'll never come to bother these horses again, Jack Egan."

Fargo shook his head. "How goddamn naive can you

146

be?" he whispered to Prudence. "The man's lied to you before."

"His life's at stake this time," she said.

"No it's not," Fargo said, and her glance was questioning. "Yours is. All he needs is words to buy new time."

Prudence took in his answer, and he saw the moment of uncertainty come into her eyes. She looked away, down at the littered passageway, and he saw her jaw stiffen again. He heard Egan's voice call out again. "What if I say go to hell?" the man said.

Fargo's voice barked the answer before Prudence found words. "I'll blow your goddamn head off, Egan," he roared. "Yours and whoever else's is left."

Prudence's quick glance carried a flash of disapproval, and she leaned forward to peer down over the edge of the narrow cut. "Give up, Jack Egan," she called. "You know you're trapped. Give up, leave here alive, and don't ever come back."

Fargo's ears picked up the sound of whispered exchanges, mutterings, a sharp curse thrown in. He gazed down, saw Egan move from behind the horse, Humphrey Wills and another man in a brown doeskin vest closeted with him. Two more gunslingers waited nearby. As he watched, the discussion ended and he saw Egan step forward, lift his face to peer upward, Humphrey Wills following his gaze. "You win, Prudence Thorpe," Egan called. "I know when I'm licked."

"Put your guns down in front of you, all of you, make a pile of them," Prudence called down, and Fargo saw Egan toss his revolver on the ground. Wills did the same, and the man in the doeskin vest put his gun with the others. He watched the two men step forward to toss their guns onto the pile. "Rifles, too," Prudence said, and Fargo saw three of the men take rifles from their saddle holsters, drop them on the ground with the revolvers. Egan lifted his hands into the air as he peered up at the girl's head visible over the edge of stone.

"That's it. I didn't carry a rifle. Neither did Mayor Wills," he said.

Prudence stood up, shot a glance of triumph at Fargo. The big man's eyes answered with cold disbelief. He backed from the edge and mounted the pinto. "You walk up here and don't take your eyes off them. Anyone tries to pick up a gun along the way, shoot him," he growled. "I'll cover them as they come out the other end." He sent the pinto racing along the top of the stone cliff and down the steep slope at the other end. He reached the ground below, his glance flicking out across the ridges and slopes of the land at the other end of the passageway. The mustangs had scattered, none in sight. He dismounted, exchanged his Colt for the big Sharps, and positioned himself half behind a tree. It was not more than a few minutes before he saw Egan climbing over the left side of the boulder where it rested against the stone wall of the passage, just enough room for a man to fit his body through.

Egan dropped to the ground when he had finished clambering over the edge of the boulder, his eyes moving in quick, searching circles. "Stay right there," Fargo called and saw the man stiffen. The gunslinger in the doeskin vest crawled from the passageway next, then Humphrey Wills and finally the two other men. Fargo stepped from behind the tree, slowly walked toward the five figures, the Colt leveled at them. His eyes found Egan's face, and he saw only cold arrogance in it. "I've a message for you, Egan," he said quietly. "You'd be dead if I'd had my way. You break your word to her and I'll come back for you. There'll be no place big enough or high enough for you to hide."

"I wouldn't go breaking my word to her, Fargo," the man said.

"You're a fucking liar," Fargo bit out. "But you remember what I just said." He stepped back, met the hate in the man's eyes with his own icy promise as Prudence rode up. Egan's eyes went to her, and Fargo let his own glance rest on Humphrey Wills. "No tricks from you or little Penny's an orphan," he growled. Wills tried to summon bluster, but the fear inside him refused, and he only looked pathetic. Fargo's glance took in the three other men. They watched impassively, and he brought his attention back to Prudence as she faced Egan.

"I've your word you'll never try to harm the mustangs again," she said.

"You've got my word," the man said too easily.

Fargo cursed silently at the believing heart. "And you've got mine," he growled and saw Egan's eyes narrow at him.

"Start walking," Prudence said firmly. "You keep going down until you can circle the mountain at the base."

Egan shot her a baleful glance as he turned to the others. "You heard the lady," he said and started to walk away. The other men filed into a straggly line behind him.

"I'll just follow them down a ways," Fargo said. "I want to be sure they don't have a change of heart."

Prudence nodded. "I'm going to ride around here a spell. The Wild Shadow's near enough. I want to find him. It's important."

He agreed with his eyes, understood what she was saying behind the simple words. She wanted to renew trust, love, the reaching out that could have been too easily shattered. She wanted to offer those things quickly, openly, before fear and suspicion took hold. He understood and silently swore again at the trust inside her. "I'll wait for you here," she said as he swung onto the pinto and let the horse slowly follow the five men as they walked down the hillside. He turned in the saddle as the

149

timberland thickened, saw her ride up to a distant ridge, and returned his gaze to the men in front of him. They walked in silence, with Wills glancing back at him frequently, his eyes taking in the big .45 Colt Fargo held in one hand.

Egan led the way, walking slowly, stepping over a fallen log and hanging onto brush as the land grew steep. Fargo halted, let the men clamber down the steep grade, and then took the pinto down sideways. The trees thinned, the land becoming almost open in a hollow, and suddenly Egan sank to the ground. Fargo halted, stayed a distance back. "Damn, I've got to rest some," Egan glared back at him. "I twisted an ankle in that damn pass."

Fargo shrugged. "Don't get any ideas or it'll be your last rest," he said with matter-of-fact calmness.

Egan shot him an angry stare. The man in the doeskin vest sat down, the other two following his example. "Goddamn, Egan, I knew I never should've signed up with you," he suddenly shouted.

"You were paid for it," Egan said, his voice rising.

"You never told us we'd have this kind of trouble," the man shouted back.

"Damn right he didn't," one of the others said.

"Jack played fair with you," Wills cut in loudly. "You're just looking to blame somebody."

Fargo felt the frown dig into his brow as the five men continued to accuse each other in loud, angry tones, the argument exploding with surprising suddenness. Or perhaps it was long-standing grievances suddenly surfacing. He was watching, the frown still on his forehead, when the shot exploded behind him. He felt the sharp pain and his temple seemed on fire. As if in a dream, he felt himself toppling from the pinto. He hit the ground sideways, rolled onto his face, and lay still. He tried to move, but his body refused to respond. He squeezed his hands, tried to move his fingers, but knew only stiffness. He wanted to pull his eyes open, and even that was impossible. He lay as if dead, aware he was not yet in that final state because he could hear, and Egan's jubilant shout came to his ears.

"Goddamn, you did it, Billy boy. And you got him, too," he heard Egan shout.

"It was my idea," he heard Wills say. "Having Billy boy play dead in the passage. You did it well, Billy. You just lay there like the others."

"You bring the guns?" Egan asked, and Fargo heard the other man grunt. Fargo felt a hand lift his head, let it drop back on the ground. He heard Egan's voice, cold rage in it. "Now we go back and finish off that rotten little bitch," the man said. "We can take care of the horses next week."

Fargo heard the sound of the footsteps moving away from him, and he cursed inside himself. He had underestimated the duplicity of both Wills and Egan. Their move had been simple and effective. One man left as dead with the others. He had only to wait and then come after them. The sudden loud argument fell into place, too, the noise used to cover the sound of the man approaching from behind. Fargo cursed again and tried to move, but he was as if dead. The bullet had hit some nerve that immobilized him, even made his breathing so shallow they'd taken him for dead. Inside himself he grunted with bitter rue. He might just as well be dead for all the help he could give Prudence. Once again, he tried to pull his eyes open and failed, and he lay with only his helpless thoughts as mocking companions.

It'd take the bastards a while to climb back up to where he'd left Prudence outside the passageway. They'd lie in wait for her to come back. There was still time, but he lay in a void where there was no time. He groaned silently, his face against the earth. He lay in the timeless suspended state and heard the sound of his own breathing. He listened and heard the shallowness lessen. He pulled his chest in and it moved and he realized his temple no longer burned with searing fire. He tried to flex his hands, felt his fingers move. *Damn.* His lips formed the word. Feeling returned to his arms. He pushed down with his hands and his arms lifted his body. The paralysis had been temporary, the nerve reacting to shock. He pushed again, drew his legs up, and they responded. He pulled his eyes open, blinked, saw the pinto standing nearby. There seemed two of the horses, and he pulled himself to his feet, shook his head. The pinto became a single horse, and he took a step toward it, collapsed onto the ground as the world spun. He lay for a moment, let his head clear, and pulled himself back on his feet. The pinto was two horses again, one overlapping the other. He headed for the center of both, stumbled, nearly fell, his hands coming into contact with warm fur and saddle leather. He hung against the horse, his hands clasped around the saddlehorn until he felt strength returning to his body.

He pulled himself into the saddle, and the forest became visible as his eyes grew clear. The Colt was still clasped in his right hand, he saw, and he managed to drop it into the holster as he sent the horse climbing upward. Every few minutes the trees seemed to double, each one becoming two, overlapping one another until they suddenly grew clear. He rode on, realized he swayed in the saddle and clung to the horn with both hands. The pinto moved up the slopes, and the trees continued to change from clear to fuzzy and back again. He used each clear interlude to strain his eyes, finally reached sight of the stone cliff and the passageway exit, and he halted the horse, let himself slide from the saddle. His vision blurred as he stepped away from the horse, and he sank down onto one knee, waited until his sight cleared. There was pressure on a nerve somewhere, he realized, intermittent pressure no doubt aggravated by moving. But he pressed forward. He'd no other choice. It was slow going, as he halted each time his vision blurred, only moved forward when it cleared. He neared the land in front of the passage exit and dropped onto his stomach and began to inch his way forward. He halted as vision blurred again, rested with his forehead pressed to the grass, moved on as his vision came clear.

He drew nearer to the passageway exit and halted, strained his eyes to sweep the area. The effort provoked a faint pounding in his temple, and he almost missed the two men beside an alder. But he saw them, let his gaze go back past the two figures until he spotted the man in the doeskin vest crouched beside another tree. That left three, he muttered under his breath, Egan, Wills and the one who had played dead. They were near, he knew, and he cursed in silent rage as the scene began to grow furry, the trees joining together. He rested his forehead on the grass again and waited. The minutes seemed like hours, but his vision grew clear finally and he raised his head in time to see Prudence riding into view, moving slowly with an almost dreamy little smile on her face. She had found the great stallion, he knew. Prudence halted, dismounted, patted the chestnut's neck, and had started to walk forward when the man moved from the trees, the six-gun in his hand. As he did so, the other two came forward, and Fargo saw Prudence's eyes grow round in astonishment. She started to turn, reach back for the rifle in the saddle holster.

"Don't try it, sister," the man rasped, and Prudence froze, slowly turned her back to him. One of the other two darted forward and yanked the rifle from its case. Fargo lifted himself onto one knee, pulled the Colt from its holster, waited, and saw Jack Egan step into view, Humphrey Wills behind him. The one they had called

Billy trailed into the clear as Egan walked up to Prudence. With a quick, savage motion, he smashed his hand across her face. She staggered backward, and he followed with a backhand blow. She fell to the ground, one hand raised to protect herself. Her eyes darted past Egan, swept the ground.

"Don't be lookin' for him," Egan snarled. "He's dead, the big bastard, dead as a doornail."

Prudence spit words at Egan. "Murderer. Rotten, stinking murderer, that's all you are."

Egan reached for her, yanked her to her feet. "Goddamn bitch. I wanted you alive when I killed those goddamn Arabians of yours. I wanted you to know it, let it tear you apart, watch you shrivel and die from inside out," he snarled. "But it'll have to be different now. I'll see you dead, first." He smashed her across the face again, and she refused to flinch. "But I want you to know that I'm going to slaughter every goddamn one of them. I'm comin' back and I'll run down every damn one." He tossed his head back, and his laugh was a twisted sound. He shook Prudence. "You hear me, bitch? You understand me? I'm going to slaughter every last one of them. Know it, take it to your grave with you, rot in hell with it. Now, what do you think about that?"

Fargo saw Prudence answer, her knee come up and kick forward. The blow was not fully on target but was hard enough to make Egan gasp, pull his hand from her, and double up in pain. He sank to the ground, and she whirled, ran, but the man in the doeskin vest cut in front of her, seized her arm, and swung her in a short arc. She landed hard on the ground, and he put his foot against her neck.

Fargo saw Egan pull himself onto one knee, his face still drawn with pain. "Just hold her . . . hold her," Egan said between harsh breaths. "I'm goin' to make her wish she was dead before I kill her."

Fargo's eyes swept the six men. They made poor targets, standing too far apart to take in with one volley of closely spaced shots. As he watched, the two other men came up and yanked Prudence to her feet. Fargo saw Egan slowly, painfully pull himself to his feet, his mouth a snarl of fury. Only five of them had guns, Fargo saw, Egan being the one without a weapon. The man started toward Prudence, and Fargo raised the Colt. He couldn't wait any longer for them to make better targets. He chose the man with the doeskin vest first, aimed, squeezed the trigger, and he was already swinging the Colt a fraction to the right as the man's ear disintegrated, a hole that seemed to explode from inside out, replacing the left side of his head. His next two shots slammed into the two men holding Prudence. One catapulted backward as though pulled by invisible wires. The other spun completely around and Prudence fell backward, screamed as his lungs sent red bursting from the hole in his chest. Fargo whirled to fire at Wills and the man called Billy, then he saw the figures become double, blur into amorphous shapes. He dived sideways, hit the ground and rolled, gasping at the sharp pain that shot through his temple. He heard the gunfire and Egan's voice. "Goddamn . . . kill him . . . Jesus, he's alive. Kill the bastard," the man screamed. Fargo rolled into tall brush as he heard three shots thud into the earth inches away. He shook his head and managed to make out the two blurred figures running toward him.

He was cursing in frustrated helplessness as he fired. Through fogged eyes he saw one figure vanish and heard the guttural gasp of pain. He flung himself sideways as two more shots whistled past him, the second fuzzy shape still coming at him. He had been lucky with the last shot. Maybe he'd be lucky twice. He raised the Colt and fired, heard the hollow sound of the hammer clicking on an empty chamber. He dived backward as another shot exploded, and he felt the heat of it cross his cheek. He twisted, slammed into a tree, and bounced off. He felt his ankle twist, and he gasped out with the pain that shot up through his leg as he sprawled on the ground. He peered upward, and the figure almost on top of him was suddenly sharply outlined, Humphrey Wills, his face twisted in snarling triumph.

Fargo drew his arm back and flung the big Colt into the man's face. He saw the hawk nose spout blood, and Wills stumbled and fell inches away from him. Fargo leaped at Wills, powerful hands outstretched to seize the man's neck. Wills brought his gun up, and Fargo closed one hand around the man's forearm, pressed it back and up. He tried to push the man onto his back and almost screamed as his ankle shot fiery shafts of pain through him. He slipped, fell, and Wills wrested his arm free, tried to bring the gun around to fire. Fargo met the man's arm with his forearm, as a boxer blocks a round-house right. The sharp jar resulted in a shot that went harmlessly into the air. Fargo drove a hard, straight blow to the jaw in front of him, and Wills went backward but clung to the gun.

Prepared for the pain of his twisted ankle, Fargo steeled himself and pushed forward after Wills, came down half atop him. Once again, the man tried to bring the gun into position, this time coming in from the side. Fargo's hand slammed down on the man's wrist, drove his arm against his chest, and Wills grunted in pain. He tried to raise the gun, and Fargo's hand closed around the trigger, blanketing Wills's fingers. He ducked as the gun went off, a hot blast brushing his forehead, and Humphrey Wills went limp, like a taut lariat suddenly cut loose. Fargo looked up. Humphrey Wills had no face, only a jumbled mass of red and crumpled bone.

He pushed himself away from the apparition and heard Prudence scream. He reached down, tore the gun from the man's lifeless fingers. It was empty, the last bullet spent, and he flung it aside as he pulled himself to his feet, started forward, almost collapsed on his swollen, twisted ankle. He saw Prudence running, circling, trying to stay away from Egan, and in the man's hand a knife blade glinted. Fargo ran forward, an agonizingly slow run, dragging his ankle behind him, almost falling twice. His eyes continued to stay clear as though, in mockery, he was being allowed to see Egan plunge the knife into Prudence.

His curses came on harsh breaths as he dragged himself forward, and he saw Prudence turn, try to race away. Egan was faster, closed the distance between himself and her running figure in seconds. Fargo saw Prudence turn, stumble, fall, twist away from one blow, and he heard Egan screaming in insensate rage. He was too far away to do anything but watch, and he felt the helplessness shrivel his gut. Prudence managed to avoid another sweeping blow of the knife, but she was already trading on borrowed time, saved so far only by Egan's wildness. Then Fargo's ears caught the sound, the ground shaking with it, and he saw the huge black form come racing into view, charging at a full-out gallop from the slope behind the two struggling figures.

Egan turned to see the horse bearing down on him. He raised the knife, decided better of it, and flung himself to the side as the ebony stallion raced past him. The horse raced on a half-dozen yards before he slowed enough to turn, and Fargo saw Egan charging at Prudence again, his face a mask of twisted fury, his only purpose to have his final victory. The stallion bolted forward again, and Fargo saw Egan halt, crouch, wait for the horse to charge past him once more. But the stallion swerved, and Egan saw the motion, flung himself sideways again, but not fast enough. The stallion slammed into his legs, and Fargo saw Egan's body arc through the air to land with a thud. The stallion wheeled, came in again, and Fargo saw Egan half rise, his face change from snarling fury to consuming terror. The stallion reared up on his hind legs, blotting out the sun, and Egan lifted his arms up in front of his face. The tremendous forelegs drove the horse's hooves downward, crashing through Egan's arms as though they were matchsticks. One hoof crashed into the man's face, obliterating it, the other smashed his skull in. Egan's figure collapsed on the ground, and the stallion came down again with both forefeet, and Fargo heard the splintering sound of chest and ribs being crushed. The horse wheeled, kicked out with powerful hind legs, and Jack Egan's body sailed into the air as though it were a broken rag doll to land behind a cluster of high brush.

The stallion wheeled again, lifted his great head, and blew air out through flared nostrils, a trumpeting of victory and of justice. Fargo dragged himself forward again and saw Prudence rise, move to the stallion's side, lean her head against the powerful chest, and Fargo halted, stayed back. It was a moment more than private, a renewal of love given and returned, an understanding fashioned of special threads only the wild in spirit could know. He felt suddenly grateful to be able to comprehend a part of it.

The stallion backed away finally, turned, and majestically moved out of sight, and Prudence slowly came to him. He sank down on one knee, his ankle throbbing unmercifully, and she gathered his head against her breasts. "You told me not to trust him," she murmured.

"So I did," he agreed.

"I should have listened to you," she said. "About everything."

He smiled into the softness of her breasts. "Yes," he murmured, his lips touching one tiny tip that pushed against her shirt.

"Let me make up for it," she whispered.

"Why not?" he said. There'd be time enough to go on later. How often did one hold the wild in spirit? How often did one ride the wild shadow?

LOOKING FORWARD

**The following is the opening section
from the next novel in the exciting
Trailsman series from Signet:**

The Trailsman #18:
CRY THE CHEYENNE

*The Cheyenne land, north of Medicine Bow,
where the Horse Creek River crosses
into the Nebraska territory.*

The big man with the lake-blue eyes surveyed the
carnage with a face that seemed carved out of stone, a
chiseled, handsome, intense face. He stood apart from
the others, had ridden over the hillock only a few minutes before the cavalry troop had reached the spot. The
girl and the old man had come along later, and the big,
black-haired man's eyes moved slowly over the scene, the
bodies that lay on the ground like so many battered doll
figures, arms and legs askew, some half draped over the
sides of the two charred Conestoga wagons. He made a
sour face, and the disgust stabbed into the pit of his
stomach.

He had seen it too many times, knew the look of it,
the feel of it, the smell of it. This was the same but
different, and he turned his eyes to the cavalry patrol, a
ten-man troop all shine and polish, including their
young faces. The lieutenant picked his way amid the
stink of death, his face held stiff. The big, black-haired

man had seen the lieutenant before, too, just as he had viewed the scene before. Other times and other places. The same but different, he grunted silently once again. The young officer was made of stiff formality, newly weaned on army manuals and rulebook tactics, long on new learning and short on old wisdom.

The big man's eyes sought out the girl. Good-looking, she was, he noted, hair the color of new wheat, eyes a soft, misty blue, an almost pert nose, nice mouth with the lower lip fuller than the upper. She wore the new-wheat hair pulled back, but it made her face more girlish than severe the way pulled-back hair did with most women. Her lime shirt pushed out in smooth fullness, and she sat her gray mare with ease. He saw her grow ashen when she rode up and thought she was going to be sick. Not that he'd have blamed her. The men were riddled with arrows, their bodies resembling pincushions. The women lay half naked, legs stretched wide, thighs smeared with blood and dirt where they'd been used before being killed. Five children lay with their heads bashed in. But the girl has pulled herself together and faced the scene, and he gave her credit for that.

His eyes swung from the girl as he heard the lieutenant's voice call out. "When did you say you got here, mister?" the officer asked.

"Five minutes before you did," the big man answered.

The lieutenant squatted down beside a lifeless form both bloodied and shot through with arrows. "What's your name, mister?" he asked without looking up.

"Fargo," the big man replied.

The lieutenant stood up and bit out his words. "The rotten, murdering savages," he said.

"The Cheyenne?" Fargo heard the girl ask.

"Of course," the lieutenant snapped grimly.

"No."

The big man let the single word drop softly from his lips and saw the others turn to him. The girl's eyes studied him, the lieutenant frowning. "No?" the young officer echoed. "Of course it was the Cheyenne. You don't know much about Indians, do you, mister?" he said.

"I know enough, more than I want to know," Fargo said almost wearily.

"Then I suggest you learn some more. These are Cheyenne arrows with Cheyenne markings on them, Indian pony tracks all over the ground," the lieutenant said. He reached down, picked up a piece of torn pouch, a design cut into it. "And this carries a Cheyenne design pattern," he said, unable to keep from sounding smugly paternal. "The Cheyenne, no doubt about it. The stinking, bloodthirsty savages," he added darkly.

Fargo let a long sigh push from his powerful chest. "No," he said wearily and turned to his horse, a stunning Ovaro, jet-black fore and hind quarters, a gleaming white midsection.

"The Cheyenne, Fargo," he heard the lieutenant call. "You'd better learn your Indians if you want to ride this territory and keep your scalp."

"Yes, sir, lieutenant, I'll work on it," Fargo said as he pulled himself onto the Ovaro. He saw the girl's mist-blue eyes watching him, a tiny furrow crossing her brow. He touched the brim of his hat to her as he turned the horse. The lieutenant shot a glance at the sun starting to dip over the horizon. "I'll leave a two-man guard overnight. It's too late to get a burial detail out here now. We'll tend to it in the morning," Fargo heard him say to the girl. "You need an escort back, Miss Jody?"

"No," the girl answered. Jody, Fargo muttered silently. It fit her, a good, no-nonsense name, strong yet feminine.

He let the pinto amble slowly away and felt the girl's eyes following him. On the other side of the hillock the scene of death was out of sight. Only the smell of charred wood followed him. He frowned as he slowly rode across the rabbitbrush-studded land. Strange, he grunted to himself, but he rode on. He'd no taste for getting into it, whatever it was. He'd gone but a quarter of a mile or so, his eyes scanning the land to find a place for the night before the sun went down, when he heard the hoof-beats coming up fast behind him. He turned in the saddle to see the girl, the old man following behind on an old horse. Fargo continued to walk the pinto slowly until she reined up alongside him. Her soft, mist-blue eyes could turn sharp, he saw, as she studied him, watched her take in his intense, chiseled handsomeness with approval.

"You still hold to what you said back there?" she asked. He nodded. "Why?" she prodded.

"My reasons," he answered.

"Let's hear them," she said.

He shook his head. "I said my piece."

"You said one word, no reasons, nothing else," she corrected him tartly.

"I'm not getting into it more," he said calmly. He let a small smile edge his lips as he took in her bristling dissatisfaction with him. "How come you followed me all the way here to ask that? Don't you believe the lieutenant? He had a whole passel of reasons," Fargo said.

"He did," she snapped. "Lieutenant Richardson is a bright fine young officer."

"You know him," Fargo grunted.

"Yes, I do," she said. "Frankly, I don't know why I

followed you. Something about you, about the way you said that one word."

"It didn't impress the lieutenant any," Fargo commented.

"Maybe it shouldn't have impressed me, either," she tossed at him. "Maybe Lieutenant Richardson was right about your having a lot to learn."

"Maybe." Fargo smiled pleasantly. The furrow on her brow had become an angry frown. But she remained one very good-looking package.

"Are you going to give me a reason, dammit?" she snapped.

"I read the wind," he said.

She pulled the gray mare in a tight circle. "Bastard," she threw back as she cantered away. The old man, a lined, narrow face on a spare, narrow body, followed after her at once. Fargo smiled as he thought about the girl. Mist-blue eyes had a banked fire behind them. She'd be worth the knowing, and he wondered why she was so interested in what had happened. More than the usual, passing interest in the violence of this land. It was the Cheyenne land, he knew, and the Cheyenne could make savagery into a fine art. But he'd not get into it more. He had things to do, appointments to keep.

The dusk was nearly night, and he rode to a stand of white cedar and halted, unsaddled the pinto, and laid out his bedroll. The night stayed warm, and he undressed to his shorts, placed the holster with the big Colt .45 in it alongside him. His hand rested lightly on it as he turned on his side and quickly slept, the rolling prairie stretching out below him and the distant call of a wolf his lullaby.

Fargo had long ago learned to sleep like the mountain cat, his subconscious forever alert, intuition and instinct awake just below his dulled surface senses. His eyes were still closed and he felt the dawn wind when it came, let himself return to sleep awhile longer. Then he woke, unmoving, his eyes snapping open. He listened to the silence, heard it broken by the sound of a horse, the faint jingle of rein chains. No Cheyenne pony, he grunted, but his hand slowly drew the Colt from the holster. He turned and rose on one elbow, the big Colt ready to fire. He saw the gray mare moving up the incline toward the cedars. The gun was still in his hand when the girl halted before him, new-wheat hair pale gold in the early sun. He saw her eyes travel across his hard-muscled body, linger on the powerful deltoid muscles, linger longer on the flat, hard abdomen where it disappeared into his shorts.

" 'Morning, Jody," he said evenly and saw the surprise in her eyes. "That's what Lieutenant Richardson called you," Fargo said.

"It's Jody," she said, almost smiled. "You can put the gun away," she said.

He nodded, leaned over, and returned the Colt to the holster. He pushed himself to his feet and watched her eyes move over his near-naked body again. "You come out here at dawn to ask questions again?" he said. "You'll be getting the same answers."

"I don't think so," she said as he pulled on trousers. He looked up from buttoning his pants to see the heavy Dragoon Colt in her hand. "Move away from your holster," she said.

He eyed the gun in her grip. "You don't want to play with those things, honey," he said soothingly. "They can go off."

"I know how to make them go off," she said. "Move aside." He obeyed, and she dismounted, kept the gun steady on him. She scooped up his gunbelt and slung it around her saddlehorn. "Finish dressing," she ordered.

"What the hell's in you?" Fargo asked as he pulled on his shirt.

"Those wagons," she said. "You're going back there with me right now, before the lieutenant's burial detail gets there. Saddle up."

He lifted his saddle, put it on the Ovaro. "Why?" he asked.

"You're going to show me why you said it wasn't the Cheyenne," she snapped.

"Thought you'd decided the lieutenant was right about my not knowing anything," Fargo said.

"You know, damn you," she threw back. "You know. I can feel it inside." He threw a glance at her. The big Dragoon Colt hadn't wavered a fraction, and he swung up on the Ovaro. She moved the gray mare a few paces behind him. "Let's go," she said. "You're going to give me reasons, chapter and verse. No bullshit about reading the wind this time."

He shrugged. He'd tell her the truth. He'd give her that much. She had the guts to follow through on her intuition, and he could admire that. He watched the dawn sun lift over the horizon, tossed her a smile. "The early bird gets the answers," he said. Her eyes softened, but he saw that she kept the gun steady. He hurried along the flatland, and the hillock came into sight. He saw her draw a deep breath and follow after him.

JOIN THE <u>TRAILSMAN</u> READER'S PANEL
AND PREVIEW NEW BOOKS

If you're a reader of <u>TRAILSMAN</u>, New American Library wants to bring you more of the type of books you enjoy. For this reason we're asking you to join <u>TRAILSMAN</u> Reader's Panel, to preview new books, so we can learn more about your reading tastes.

Please fill out and mail today. Your comments are appreciated.

1. The title of the last paperback book I bought was:_____

2. How many paperback books have you bought for yourself in the last six months?
☐ 1 to 3   ☐ 4 to 6   ☐ 10 to 20   ☐ 21 or more

3. What other paperback fiction have you read in the past six months? Please list titles:_____
_____
_____
_____

4. I usually buy my books at: (Check One or more)
☐ Book Store   ☐ Newsstand   ☐ Discount Store
☐ Supermarket   ☐ Drug Store   ☐ Department Store
☐ Other (Please specify)_____

5. I listen to radio regularly: (Check One)   ☐ Yes   ☐ No
My favorite station is:_____
I usually listen to radio (Circle One or more)   On way to work /
During the day / Coming home from work / In the evening

6. I read magazines regularly: (Check One) ·   ☐ Yes   ☐ No
My favorite magazine is:_____

7. I read a newspaper regularly: (Check One)   ☐ Yes   ☐ No
My favorite newspaper is:_____
My favorite section of the newspaper is:_____

For our records, we need this information from all our Reader's Panel Members.
NAME:_____
ADDRESS:_____ ZIP_____
TELEPHONE: Area Code (   ) Number_____

8. (Check One)   ☐ Male   ☐ Female

9. Age (Check One)   ☐ 17 and under   ☐ 18 to 34
☐ 35 to 49   ☐ 50 to 64   ☐ 65 and over

10. Education (Check One)
☐ Now in high school   ☐ Graduated high school
☐ Now in college   ☐ Completed some college
☐ Graduated college

As our special thanks to all members of our Reader's Panel, we'll send a free gift of special interest to readers of <u>THE TRAILSMAN</u>.

Thank you. Please mail this in today.

NEW AMERICAN LIBRARY
PROMOTION DEPARTMENT
1633 BROADWAY
NEW YORK, NY 10019